DEATH IN DESPAIR

THE BODY of a drunken furniture dealer found drowned in a canal and that of a defaulting cashier found shot in the vault of a London bank, seemed to have no connection whatever and the coroners at the respective inquests found verdicts of accidental death and suicide quite in keeping with the circumstances of each. The information supplied by a dying teddy-boy to a priest, however, made further investigations necessary and Superintendent Littlejohn, of Scotland Yard, found himself involved in a case which alternated between the oily waters of a canal near Berkhampstead and the urbane precincts of a bank in Moorgate. The kindly Superintendent learned quite a lot about inland navigation and finance before he solved the affair.

George Bellairs has also written:

LITTLEJOHN ON LEAVE
FOUR UNFAITHFUL SERVANTS
DEATH OF A BUSYBODY
DEAD SHALL BE RAISED
TURMOIL IN ZION
MURDER OF A QUACK
HE'D RATHER BE DEAD
CALAMITY AT HARWOOD
DEATH IN THE NIGHT WATCHES
CRIME AT HALFPENNY BRIDGE
THE CASE OF THE SCARED RABBITS
DEATH ON THE LAST TRAIN
OUTRAGE ON GALLOWS HILL
THE CASE OF THE SEVEN WHISTLERS
THE CASE OF THE FAMISHED PARSON
THE CASE OF THE DEMENTED SPIV
THE CASE OF THE HEADLESS JESUIT
DEAD MARCH FOR PENELOPE BLOW
DEATH IN DARK GLASSES
CRIME IN LEPERS' HOLLOW
A KNIFE FOR HARRY DODD
HALF-MAST FOR THE DEEMSTER
CORPSES IN ENDERBY
THE CURSING STONES MURDER
DEATH IN ROOM FIVE
DEATH TREADS SOFTLY
DEATH DROPS THE PILOT
DEATH IN HIGH PROVENCE
DEATH SENDS FOR THE DOCTOR
CORPSE AT THE CARNIVAL
MURDER MAKES MISTAKES
BONES IN THE WILDERNESS
TOLL THE BELL FOR MURDER
DEATH IN THE FEARFUL NIGHT

" Our own George Bellairs with his highly individual blend of the gay and the factual."

FRANCIS ILES of the *Guardian.*

Death in Despair

by George Bellairs

THE THRILLER BOOK CLUB
121 CHARING CROSS ROAD
LONDON W.C.2

First published 1960

© George Bellairs 1960

This is a work of fiction, the characters are entirely
imaginary, and no reference is made or intended to
any person, alive or dead

Printed in Great Britain by
Northumberland Press Limited
Gateshead on Tyne

CONTENTS

1

THE CONSCIENCE OF ALFIE BATT

THE END OF June and magnificent weather in London. There had been a succession of fine, hot days and the sun still burned down, making the streets shimmer with the heat and anything solid almost too hot to touch. Littlejohn closed the file he had been reading in his room at Scotland Yard, took off his spectacles, and went and stood at the open window. On the Embankment nobody was hurrying. Even the passing traffic on the river seemed to be moving more slowly than usual. Holidaymakers wearing a minimum of light clothing; women in flowered summer frocks, men carrying their coats and some even wearing straw hats. The pavement artist who sat opposite the great gates of New Scotland Yard and who greeted Littlejohn every morning, had, from somewhere, secured a grubby alpaca jacket and an old panama and was lolling with his back to the wall. In such a world of sunlight the dark figure which detached itself from behind a group of sightseers following a guide, seemed particularly incongruous. Under the glare of sunshine, it was like a black shadow crossing the road. An enormous Roman Catholic priest.

Cromwell entered and stood with Littlejohn at the window.

" Hot, isn't it? "

Had anyone other than Cromwell said it, Littlejohn would have felt irritated. It was on everybody's lips. Some even made it into a sort of resentful greeting, as though they were fed-up with the heat. Then, when it rained, they'd complain that the weather had let them down.

" Is that Father Silvester? " said Cromwell, leaning across the sill and following the progress of the large sombre figure. " He looks to be coming here."

" Yes. Something else wrong in Lambeth."

Father Silvester, a priest in a very shady quarter across the river, was one of Littlejohn's good friends. Now and then, when he was in difficulties with unruly members of his flock, he called at the Yard for help or advice. It was obvious that he was on his way to the Superintendent now.

" Will you need me for a bit? "

Many of the personnel were away on holidays and, judging from the number of new cases on the records, most of the criminals were away, too, doing business at the seaside; the lowly ones at home resorts, the high-ups on the Riviera or yachting on the Mediterranean. Cromwell's wife and family had gone to his mother-in-law's in Cornwall, where he proposed to join them in a few days' time. Littlejohn had invited him to stay with them in Hampstead, but Cromwell had politely declined as he was decorating his flat in his solitude. He was eager to get away and mix himself some more paint.

" I don't think so, old chap. Go and get on with your decorating. Which room is it today? The mushroom and grey . . . ? "

An orderly entered.

" Could Father Silvester have a word with you, sir? "

It would probably be an hour's job, but the orderly was a north-countryman and in the habit of making massive understatements.

" Show him in, please, and have some tea sent up."

" Tea? "

" Yes. The Father won't drink anything else."

The orderly burst into perspiration at the mention of it.

Father Silvester was a huge man, who made even Littlejohn look small. It wasn't corpulence, but solid bone and muscle inherited from generations of powerful farmers before him. Littlejohn anxiously eyed the chairs as the priest entered. They shook hands and Father Silvester selected a seat.

" I think this is mine. . . ."

He tested the resistance of the chair by gripping the back

with his huge hand and throwing all his weight on it. Then, satisfied, he sat on it.

He had the face of a priest, and yet there was none of the austerity or religious ardour of a monk about it. It was ruddy, strong, shrewd and compassionate at the same time, and the grey eyes shone with good humour. A working priest, with well-kept useful hands and a tongue which could be kindly, witty, caustic, or comforting as the case demanded.

The tea entered.

"Sorry, I daren't invite you to take off your coat, Father, but I can offer you a cooling drink."

The attendant was pouring out the tea at arm's length to keep the heat from his face.

"Nothing I'd like better."

They drank slowly and in silence for a minute or two. Littlejohn knew the priest liked a cigar now and then and produced a box of expensive ones from his drawer. They'd been sent to him at Christmas by a forger he'd once put behind bars and who, since his release, had always remembered him kindly. "All the best for Christmas, to the man who put me straight. From Edgar the Endorser."

"May I smoke it at home tonight? It would hardly do to be seen entering the presbytery smoking a Havana. . . ."

A pause.

"You heard about the trouble down our way last night, Littlejohn?"

"The dance-hall scuffle, you mean?"

"The same . . ."

The priest put down his cup, crossed his legs, and leaned back. His chair creaked. His shoes were enormous, workman-like, and very brightly polished.

"One of the boys died."

"So I heard. An accident."

"Yes. Your men were rounding-up a few of them and this fellow, Alfie Batt, broke away, climbed up a downspout, crossed a roof, and slipped off. He impaled himself on some railings in an area below. It grieves me. He wasn't a bad lad,

A*

really. Just a bit high-spirited and too proud to be arrested like the others. He was one of *my* boys."

Many of the roughs of Father Silvester's parish still paid allegiance to him and his church. Perhaps it was because he was physically powerful and had, on occasions, broken-up street brawls single-handed; or it may have been that they admired his integrity and love of fair-play.

" I was with him when he died in St. Thomas's."

" I see. I'm sorry. Anything I can do? "

" No. It's past that now. He was conscious for about an hour, however, before he died. He asked for me. I was glad he did. He confessed his sins. They were all venial ones. He'd have grown out of them."

He emptied his cup and absent-mindedly poured himself another.

" The worst one was a bit of blackmail, which, however, had grave consequences. The man who was being black-mailed shot himself."

" A venial sin, did you say, Father? "

" Young Batt had no idea that it would all end as it did. In fact, I doubt if the blackmail was the cause of the man's death. It was probably his conscience. You see, he'd committed a murder."

" Which Alfie Batt had witnessed? "

" Yes. You shall express your opinion after I've told you what happened. This is no breach of the seal of the confessional. As the murderer had died by his own hand, I felt you ought to know the true story and clear the matter up truthfully. The verdict at the inquest of the victim was an open one. Batt agreed to my telling you."

" Thank you, sir. Could you let me know the name of the murdered man and then perhaps we can turn-up the files? "

" I don't know myself. Batt, as you will well understand, was dying and not very clear in his mind. He wanted to get it all off his conscience."

" But how did he know the verdict on his own victim was suicide? "

"Let me tell you from the beginning."

Littlejohn was busy trying to remember any cases of suicide which might recently have come his way.

"It seems that Alfie and some friends went one evening into the country near Berkhampstead. They had scooters . . . hired ones. . . ."

"Forgive me, Father. . . . When would this be?"

"In May, this year. They were a mixed party and Alfie and one of the girls, who had been pillion-riding with him, broke away from the rest, presumably to enjoy some courting by the canal, which, as you know, runs through some very pleasant places there. They eventually found themselves on the banks of a little tributary of the main water which ended in a secluded and small disused wharf. There Batt and his girl parked their vehicle and lay down in the long grass and rushes, not far from the water. I tell you this in my own words, Littlejohn. Alfie's account was frequently incoherent and I had to question him and then, at times, draw my own conclusions. It is strange how long it is taking me to tell you what Alfie contained in a few words. But then I am a Celt, use my imagination, and am inclined to a love of language. . . ."

He smiled and shrugged his great shoulders

Through the open windows came strains of music and the cheers of a crowd. It all seemed very remote from Alfie Batt's dying story and neither of the two men made any move to find out what was going on outside.

"They had been there for some time. . . . They must have found it very pleasant, for it had grown almost dark by the time they began to think of returning to London. It was then that they heard a car approaching along the disused, dilapidated road which had once carried traffic to and from the wharf. Alfie said he raised himself gently and peeped at what was going on. There wasn't a soul about, the night was not completely dark, and he thought it might be other lovers who also knew his secret retreat. But it wasn't. The car, without lights, drew-up at the wharf-head, a man got out and made sure there was nobody about. He then returned to the car, dragged out a body, and threw it in the water."

"Batt didn't interfere with what was going on?"

"No. Alfie's type are not prone to meddle in other people's business, especially when they see that it might pay handsome profits to keep quiet."

"Please go on, Father. Sorry I interrupted."

"Alfie and his friend remained unseen as this little sordid drama was played out. The body did not sink right away. This seemed to agitate the man who had brought it. He hid himself in one of the disused outbuildings of the wharf, in a position where he could see the body, finally came out when he was satisfied that it had sunk to the bottom, and then he made off along the old road again."

The priest paused as though overcome by horror at the unfolding tale.

"As soon as the car was out of sight, Alfie and his girl emerged. They took a quick look at the place where the body had been thrown in. Even as they did so, a few bubbles rose and broke on the surface of the dark water. Batt said he was sure then that the victim had not been quite dead when he was thrown in. This was his last breath."

"And still Alfie didn't try to save him?"

"He said it was useless. He couldn't swim and even if he'd dived in, it would have been too late. Instead, he and his companion quickly mounted their scooter and made off the way they'd come. As they reached the end of the track— it was rather a long one, and they, too, were without lights— the car which had brought the body was just turning into the highroad. Its lights were put on, and it made off in the direction of Watford. Alfie followed it."

"To the end of its journey?"

"Yes. It drew-up at a house on the outskirts of Barnet, and with Alfie Batt still watching, the owner of the car garaged it, went indoors, and that was all for that night, at least."

"Then, Alfie put on the squeeze?"

"Yes. He did it systematically. Next morning, early, Alfie

was again at Barnet, spying on the house. He saw a man, who very much resembled his quarry of the night before, emerge, followed him, travelled on the same train as he to London and watched him enter the Moorgate branch of the Home Counties Bank. When the bank opened, Alfie went in to change a pound note and found his man there. He was one of the tellers."

The priest poured out the rest of the tea, now cold, and sipped it.

"Shall I order more, Father?"

"No, thanks, Littlejohn. I've nearly finished."

He put down the cup.

"The rest of Alfie's business was done in the City. He found that his man lunched at an inn in Cheapside. He followed him there, sat down at the same table, and simply said 'I was on the canal-bank at Berkhampstead last night'. The squeeze, as you call it, had begun. Alfie went gently. Five pounds in two successive weeks. The man paid meekly. Then ten pounds. . . . Still without trouble. This went on for exactly a month. Then, the victim didn't turn up at the rendezvous. At two o'clock, Batt went in the bank with another pound note. His victim was there and changed it for him. Alfie passed over a slip with the pound note. 'See you outside after closing.' Alfie was at the side door at three. He thought they all went home then. It seems they didn't. Around five, the staff began to leave. Finally, most of the lights went off, the last of the staff left the building, and Alfie had not seen his man. He rang the side-door bell. There was no answer. He waited. Shortly afterwards, a woman, who might have been the caretaker, let herself in. Alfie assumed his victim had given him the slip, made up his mind to return tomorrow, and gave it up for the day."

"And then. . . ."

"Next morning, on the front page of the paper, he read that on the previous night a cashier of the Home Counties Bank, Moorgate, had shot himself in the empty office. He knew it was his man and that he perhaps had been the cause of it. Two days later, the inquest was reported. Suicide whilst the balance of his mind was deranged. The dead man had been found to be wrong in his cash."

" What was his name, Father? "

" Alfie didn't remember. He was in a sorry state when he told me his story. I suppose you could find out."

" Yes. The inquest would be . . . let me see . . . about a week ago? "

" About that."

Littlejohn rang down on the office telephone, and asked for a search in the records.

" And, at the same time, find out if any bodies were found in the Grand Union or its tributaries around Berkhampstead, please. About mid-May or afterwards."

" The address in Barnet, Father? "

" Also a blank. I don't suppose Alfie knew it. He confined his main enterprise to Moorgate after he'd nailed down his man."

" So, we don't know the name of the man who was thrown in the canal, nor the name and address of his murderer? "

" No."

" The blackmail was conducted anonymously."

" It would seem so, Littlejohn."

" You're sure that the man who committed suicide was the one Alfie was blackmailing, sir? "

" I can't say I'm sure. But it seems to me that he waited until all the rest of the staff had gone home and then killed himself. Batt was at the side door, remember, and didn't meet his man, who seems to have stayed behind for the purpose of suicide."

A constable entered with the records. There were a number of files but it proved an easy task sorting them out.

On June 23rd, the body of Cyril Bastable, a bank cashier, of Barnet, was found in the basement of the Home Counties Bank, Moorgate Branch. Bastable had shot himself with a revolver. The wound was in the chest and death must have been instantaneous. Mrs. Casabon, the

*cleaner of the office, who arrived at 6.0 p.m., found the
body. . . .*

Then, a newspaper report of the inquest.

*Suicide whilst of unsound mind. The Coroner expressed
sympathy for Bastable's wife. The deceased had, it seemed,
on the evidence of Mr. Abbott, the manager of the branch,
been wrong in his cash and had systematically defrauded
his employers of more than a thousand pounds. This must
have weighed on his mind and driven him to despair.*

"We rang up Berkhampstead police about bodies in the
canal, sir. This is a memo of the conversation."

He handed Littlejohn a typed sheet.

Only one dead body of a man recovered from the G.U.
Canal on or since mid-May. Recovered May 29th.

*Frederick Plaster. 56. Furniture Dealer, 22, Webb Street,
South Mimms.*
*Body recovered from sluice at junction of main canal and
cut to disused Waterbury Wharf.*
Had been immersed several days . . . probably four or five.
Cause of death: Drowning. Probably whilst drunk.
Heavy alcohol content in blood and stomach.
Open verdict.

"This seems to be our man, Father. Though what Bastable wanted to kill him for is a mystery. We'll have to look
into it now."

"Poor Alfie Batt seems to have stumbled into a real
hornets' nest. A murder, and then an involvement in blackmail must have driven Bastable insane. . . ."

He rose and held out his hand.

"Thank you for listening to me, Littlejohn. I've taken up
a lot of your time and greatly inflated Alfie's short and
dying account of what was on his conscience. I'll now leave
the rest to you."

" Did Alfie happen to mention the girl who was with him when he saw all this going on at the wharf, Father? "

" No. But we could soon find out, I think. He wasn't what one might call ' going steady ' with any of the girls, that I know of, but his friends in the locality—the ones who formed the Berkhampstead party which he and his girl deserted— will probably be able to tell us. You wish to see the girl? "

" Most certainly, Father. She may be able to help us quite a lot. And could you get to know from one of the gang who went, the date of the outing to Berkhampstead in May."

" I'll find out and telephone you, then, Superintendent. Good-bye, for the present."

" Good-bye, Father, and thank you."

Littlejohn went to the window again and looked out over the river. It was nearing five o'clock and the homebound traffic from the City was growing. Westminster Bridge was choc-a-bloc with vehicles. Now and then, a car loaded with luggage, and even one with a table and deck-chairs on the roof and another with fishing-rods on the top, swept along eagerly as though the occupants couldn't get to their destin- ations quickly enough. Languid crowds, most of them brim- ming with good humour in spite of the heat, trailed along the footpaths. . . .

A body found in a canal; the suicide of a bank teller. They hadn't aroused any interest. After all, holidays were in the offing and the coroners had seemed satisfied. One had even expressed his sympathy with the widow, although the bank cashier had put the body in the water before life was extinct. After all, how was the coroner to know he was a murderer.

Nobody knew the bank-man had killed the furniture- dealer from South Mimms. It needed a teddy-boy to die in hospital and tell the tale to his confessor to bring it all out.

Littlejohn looked at his watch. Too late now to enquire into it today. He'd have a wash, get home in reasonable time, and take Letty out for a run. Perhaps they'd have dinner somewhere. Berkhampstead. . . . He hadn't been there in years. He checked himself. He wouldn't think of the case again until tomorrow.

He was standing in the washroom, his shirt-sleeves rolled-up to the elbows, his arms in cold water, enjoying the cool-ness of it, wondering whether or not to make a real job of it and take a cold bath before he left.

" Sorry to disturb you, sir. Telephone."

The constable smiled pacifically at Littlejohn, as though he was sorry to spoil his fun.

" Who is it, Nicholson? "

" Father Silvester. I told him I thought you'd gone."

" Put him through down here, please."

His arms still dripping, the Superintendent took up the instrument in the ante-room.

" I thought I might catch you, Littlejohn. I found Alfie Batt's companion of the night in Berkhampstead. It was a girl called Christine Bobbitt. I have her here with me now. Can you see her tonight? "

Littlejohn almost asked him, ' What's the hurry? ' But the name Christine Bobbitt sounded intriguing. It might have been a label specially concocted to suit the type who would lie in the reeds on the canal bank with Alfie Batt for hours and hours until it was dark, see a body thrown in the canal, and forget it because Alfie told her to.

" All right, Father. Bring her in. I'll wait for you."

He filled up the washbowl with cold water, took off his collar, and thrust his head right in it. Then he dried him-self and felt a lot better.

On the way back he ordered some more tea and some sandwiches to be sent up to his room. There, he went to the window and looked out again.

Below, the Embankment was quieter. Everybody was having tea or else they were on their ways home. Then he saw the priest and his companion crossing the road. An incongruous pair, if ever there was one. A huge man in black from head to foot, his cassock flapping round his big feet. And a girl whose jet-black hair made Father Silvester's garments seem grey. She wore tight red matador jeans, what might have been a sleeveless cotton jumper—and little else. Over the jumper an unseasonable woollen lumber-jacket had been drawn. Littlejohn smiled. Father Silvester had probably told her to cover herself with something decent before she accompanied him. She was walking almost stiff-legged with defiance and people passing turned to look twice at her and wonder what sin she had committed and what the priest was going to do about it.

2

THE BARGEES' REST

"SHE HAPPENED TO be in the street, so I brought her in right away. And, by the way, the date they went to the wharf and saw the crime was May 25th."

Christine Bobbitt entered Littlejohn's room with a show of reluctance. It was not fear; just cussedness. Miss Bobbitt didn't like, as she called it, being pushed around.

She had jet-black hair, greasy, and thrust back from her face and caught-up in a pony-tail. Large dark eyes, a pale complexion, a regular rather round face, a turned-up nose and thick lips. Naturally, she might have been good-looking. But she had decorated herself with lipstick and mascara and plucked her eyebrows and painted-in false ones with a view to resembling her favourite film-star, an Italian with a large bust of which she displayed as much as she was allowed.

Christine, as she entered, removed the lumber-jacket and revealed that she was imitating the Italian in the matter of the bust as well.

"Put that back," said Father Silvester.

"It's hot in here."

"All the same, put it on again. I won't have you in my company indecently dressed."

Miss Bobbitt reluctantly obeyed. She seemed spellbound by the sheer physical power of the muscular priest.

It took them quite a time to settle down and even then it didn't result in much.

Asked to be seated, Christine did so without a word of thanks, fixed herself straddle-legged on a chair, and began to chew gum which she released from some part of her mouth. The priest made no comment. Perhaps he thought her mode of sitting was due to much pillion-riding.

" How old are you, Miss Bobbitt? "

She gave Littlejohn a queer, predatory smile. In the first place, nobody ever called her Bobbitt; in the second, she was going to ask him to guess her age.

" Tell him. And stop grinning. This is a case of murder, not a picnic."

" Sixteen."

She looked ageless. She had still the legs and gangling gait of a girl, but the torso and head of a mature woman.

" You were a friend of Alfie Batt? "

" I was his girl."

" Oh. You went with him on a scooter to Berkhampstead in the middle of May? "

" Yes. What's wrong with that? "

" And you left the rest, and the pair of you went to Waterbury Wharf and stayed there until dark."

Christine Bobbitt's eyes glowed with anger and she rose to her feet by hoisting herself up on the back of the chair.

" Who's been talking? Who was spying on us? "

The priest intervened.

" Alfie told me the night he died, Christine."

" What did he do that for? Why should he . . . ? "

" Because whilst you were there, a body was flung into the canal near where the two of you were lying. You knew that, didn't you? "

" No, I didn't. Alfie didn't tell me. He left me lyin' in the grass where I couldn't see a thing and went off to watch somebody doing somethin' on the wharf. It was nearly dark."

" And you didn't go to see what was interesting Alfie? " asked Littlejohn.

" No. Why should I? Matter of fact, I was mad with him. I thought he'd a nerve to leave me just when we were nice and cosy together, to go spyin' on other couples. I'd have left him, only it was too far back to London and I couldn't walk it."

" Did you ask what he'd been doing? "

" No. I didn't speak to him again till we got to Barnet.

He didn't speak to me, either. Then he wanted to know if I was hungry. I asked him what he thought I was after all that time. So we went an' had some supper and made it up again."

"You followed a car from Berkhampstead to Barnet?"

"Yes. Why, I didn't know."

"And Alfie didn't say why?"

"No. The car was travellin' at some speed, so Alfie had to do the same, as he seemed to want to keep up with it. He nearly had me off the back a time or two."

"You followed the car to Barnet, and what then?"

"Alfie left me with the scooter while he went to see where the fellow who had the car lived."

"Did you see the man who owned the car?"

"It was dark by the time we got to Barnet. . . ."

It was all very difficult. The girl obviously despised the police, probably for their share in the affair which had resulted in Alfie's death. She was insolent and resentful, and only there and answering questions under the will of Father Silvester. His control of this wild-cat was astonishing.

"But did you see the man?"

"I told you, it was dark. I saw him in the distance, but it was only like his shape, a sort of shadow going in the house from his garage."

"What was he like?"

"Tall."

"Is that all?"

"I said it was dark. He was tall. . . . He might have been slim. I wouldn't know."

"Did you know that Alfie was blackmailing him?"

"No. He said he'd touched him for a quid or two. . . ."

"When did he tell you that?"

"Next time we went out after we went that night to Barnet."

The memory of Alfie Batt didn't seem to trouble her at all. He might have been alive still.

"Where did you go to?"

"A scooter-run again. To Brighton. Alfie was in the

money. I never knew where he got it. Perhaps he borrowed from the man in the car."

"And Alfie never told you about the blackmail?"

"Alfie wasn't doin' no blackmail. He wasn't that sort. Can I go now? I gotta date."

"Sit where you are till the Superintendent has finished."

"But. . . ."

"Never mind your date. Is there anything more, Superintendent?"

"I don't think so, Father. If you remember anything I ought to know, Miss Bobbitt, tell Father Silvester."

The girl rose and smoothed out her matador pants. Then she stood for a minute, chewing her gum, like a ruminant animal.

"Could tell you somethin' right now. . . . Alfie was scared of somebody."

"Why didn't you say so before?"

"Never asked me."

She chewed away nonchalantly.

"Whom was he scared of?"

"I don't know. It wasn't the police. No copper ever scared Alfie. And it wasn't the coppers made him climb to the roof when he fell off. . . ."

"Who, then?"

"I don't know. Somebody was after Alfie."

"Was he scared of the man he was blackmailing?"

"I don't know. . . ."

"But that man had taken his own life before Alfie died. So it could not have been he, Littlejohn," said the priest.

"Had Alfie lost his nerve?"

"Yes. He was scared."

Littlejohn turned to the priest.

"Did he say anything of that to you, Father?"

"No. He didn't finish . . . He rambled off in his statement and died. . . . I didn't let him finish. He was in such a state that I had to begin to give him the comfort of the church. . . . You follow?"

"I do, Father."

" And he never told you who'd scared him, Miss Bobbitt? "

" Stop callin' me Miss Bobbitt. I'd never hear the last of it."

" Very well, Christine. . . . When did he seem to get scared? "

" After the night we went to *The Bargees' Rest*."

" What is that, a pub? "

" A sort of garden where you can get drinks. It's on the bank of a canal. I remember the name because my dad was a bargee. He was always resting, too. . . . Taking a holiday on the dole."

" Where is this place? "

" In the direction we went before; the night we went to Barnet."

" Berkhampstead? "

" I don't know. Alfie took me on the scooter. He made me stay with it while he took a look round. When he'd gone, I went and took a look round, too. He wasn't orderin' me about and havin' me parking myself like an old car."

" And this *Bargees' Rest*? "

" People were sittin' having drinks and there was a sort of open-air bar there, too."

" What kind of people? "

" All sorts. Toffs in shorts and white shirts. One of them had a navy-cap on. . . . Then there were some ordinary people just havin' a beer. Some had come in boats, like people do on canals. Catch me with a boat on a canal. Crawlin' about at five miles an hour. It 'ud bore me stiff."

" You don't know where it is? Could you find it again? "

" No. I didn't even know which canal it was. Somewhere off the roads north."

" Did Alfie spot you when you followed him? "

" Not likely. If he'd . . . He'd a temper and could get rough. I saw him peeping round the back of the place as if he might be searching for somebody. I went back to the scooter and he came soon after. He looked a bit upset. He hardly spoke all the way home."

" Right. Now tell me, Christine, what caused the row the night Alfie was killed? "

" A gang of fellows came to the Ritz. We were dancing. They were after Alfie."

" Is that what he was afraid of? "

" He wasn't scared of any gangs."

" What happened? "

" Some of our boys told them they didn't like the look of their faces. That started it. There was a fight in the street. Alfie was in with the rest of the boys. Then, suddenly, he broke away and started to climb the pipe to get away. . . ."

" Why? "

" He must have seen somebody, or else been tipped-off."

" Was he trying to escape from the police? "

" No fear. I don't know who it was. We never found out where those boys come from. They all got away, of course. The police pinched two of ours. That's all I know."

" You've asked round if anybody knew the strangers? "

" Of course. So have the boys. They want to find out. And when they do . . . they'll pay them a return visit."

" If they do, you'll let me know."

" What, and let the police be there before them! "

" We'll let you know, Superintendent," said the priest and led the girl away, still meekly protesting about the weight of her lumber-jacket.

Littlejohn looked at his watch. Half-past six. Too late for the bank. Then his eye caught his desk calendar. June 29th. One of the dates on which banks sometimes worked. " Balance ", they called it. Putting on and taking off interest and charging commission for work they'd done over the half-year.

" See if you can get me the manager of the Home Counties Bank, Moorgate Branch, please."

The telephone operator seemed surprised.

" They close at three, sir."

" All the same, just try."

It worked. A suave voice at the other end.

"Abbott here. I'm afraid there's nothing I can do for you now. We're closed and the cash is locked-up."

"This is Superintendent Littlejohn, New Scotland Yard, sir."

Ten minutes later, Littlejohn was on his way to the City in a police-car.

"Nothing wrong, I hope," said the manager.

"Just a little help, if you can give it, sir. It's about the late Mr. Bastable."

The place seemed new, built on contemporary lines, with plenty of unpolished mahogany and glass. The manager's room was sumptuous. Thick carpet, elegant furniture, panelling all carefully matched and arranged. Mr. Abbott made Littlejohn comfortable and gave him a cigar and a glass of sherry. He might have been a client asking for a large overdraft against boundless security.

Outside, in the main office, the staff were still working. Without the public, it had a hollow sound and the machines and footsteps echoed round the majestic chandeliers suspended from the ornamental ceiling. Mr. Abbott didn't seem to be doing much. There was a tray of consumed tea and cakes on his desk and the evening paper which he had laid aside when Littlejohn had been brought to him. Probably he was killing time as he anxiously waited for the half-year's results.

"Poor Bastable. If only he'd confided in me instead of taking his own life. It's been a great shock to us all. He was such a nice fellow. I never would have thought it of him."

"Married?"

"Yes. A nice wife. They'd no children. Which might be described as a mercy in the circumstances."

"What age, sir?"

"Fifty. He'd been here about seven years."

"A teller, I believe."

"Second cashier. In charge of the cash when the chief cashier is absent."

"His cash was wrong?"

Mr. Abbott contemplated a nightmare.

"Yes. A thousand pounds. Certainly very serious and it must have preyed on his mind. It must have occurred within three or four weeks of his death. I personally checked his cash and found it in order, as regulations provide, only four weeks before and the Inspectors from Head Office did so a couple of months before that. I just can't understand what he had been doing."

Mr. Abbott drank the dregs of his abandoned teacup absentmindedly, realized what he was doing, and thrust the cup away in disgust.

"Was Bastable a spendthrift?"

"Not to my knowledge. He seemed to live quietly. He was interested in amateur theatricals in the winter and in boating on the canal, near Berkhampstead, in the summer when they weren't rehearsing plays. But one never knows. He seemed to spend all the salary he earned in the bank. He didn't save much. His account here shows that. There may have been other things. . . ."

"Such as, sir?"

"The usual causes of a man's ruin. . . . Living above one's income; running another woman; betting; stock exchange gambling; racing . . . No traces of which appear at all in the account of Bastable here. Of course, they wouldn't. He'd keep such matters away from his account with us, wouldn't he? But he had none of the appearances of irregular living."

"What does a theft of a thousand pounds all in one sum suggest, sir?"

"A moneylender, of course. Perhaps he'd got in the clutches of one of them, who threatened to disclose the fact to the bank. I've heard of that happening."

Perhaps that was where the little drowned man from South Mimms came in!

"Was he sociable with his colleagues?"

"Yes. They got on very well together. This unfortunate affair has come as a great grief and shock to us all. Myers, the accountant here, and Falconer, our chief cashier, were particular friends of the Bastables and have taken it very badly. They've been awfully kind to his widow."

" What is Mrs. Bastable doing at present? "

" She is with her mother, who lives at Brighton. She was quite prostrated. A highly-strung woman to start with. They had to get a doctor in to her after they broke the news."

"The cleaner found the body?"

"Yes. . . . Mrs. Casabon. Most unfortunate. Her husband committed suicide by hanging some years ago. She seems to be unlucky."

A shadow appeared on the opaque glass in the door of Mr. Abbott's room and he rose to see who it was. A clerk with some figures. Mr. Abbott sent him away for the time being, much to his surprise, for they were the profits!

" May I ask why Scotland Yard have been brought into this matter, Superintendent? "

Mr. Abbott looked worried. He was a tall, well-built man of fifty or thereabouts, with thin fair hair, a rosy face, and horn-rimmed spectacles. Talking of the recent tragedy seemed to upset him, for, as he asked his question of Littlejohn, he grew haggard, as though anticipating further trouble.

Littlejohn was anxious, as yet, not to cause alarm by making public the affair at Waterbury Wharf. The shock which the respectable Bastable had caused by shooting himself in the bank was quite enough for the present, without divulging his business with a dead body in a remote reach of the canal.

" The other night, sir, a teddy-boy died in a street brawl in Lambeth and mentioned the suicide at this office to the priest who was at his deathbed. The matter is somewhat obscure, but we think we had better look further into the affairs of the late Mr. Bastable."

" How strange! The last man in the world to have dealings with such a person. Bastable was a quiet, rather melancholy type, and I've never heard of his being bold enough to associate with violent people. However, you know best, Superintendent, and I do assure you that you will have the fullest co-operation of myself and everyone else here in your investigations. It may be that something will come to light which may help solve the matter of Bastable's defalcations. It may even clear his name. I hope so. We were very fond of him. Which makes it all the more difficult, seeing that his cash was wrong and only found to be so after his death."

"I would like to call at a more convenient time, sir, and talk to some of Mr. Bastable's old colleagues about him. It's late now and I'm sure you want to be getting finished and off home. . . ."

"Don't let that deter you, Superintendent. But, Falconer has already gone, and Myers is putting the finishing touches to the half-year's results. It would be better if you could come tomorrow, if convenient. Say, eleven in the morning. They will all be available then."

"Very good, sir. That should be fine. I'll confirm it by telephone before I leave the Yard. Do you live anywhere near Bastable's old home?"

"Not very far away, as the crow flies. Uxbridge. There's a bunch of us live in the vicinity. Myers lives at South Mimms, and Falconer at New Barnet. It's easily explained. Bastable lived at Barnet and when Falconer arrived from one of our branches in the north, he and Bastable became good friends and Falconer used to visit the Bastables whilst he was looking for a house. Eventually, he came upon a place in New Barnet through being familiar with the neighbourhood. Myers is a South Mimms man. Never lived anywhere else. The three families were all associated with the local dramatic society and, through Myers, who's a keen sailor, spent a lot of time in the summer running motor-launches on the canal. In fact, there has been quite an epidemic of canal sailing. Myers has fired some of our younger men with enthusiasm. We call it the Moorgate Navy. There are about seven of them, all told, boating on the Grand Union."

"Including yourself, sir?"

"No. I'm a golfer. But I've been down there with the crowd. It's very pleasant on a sunny evening or week-end. There's a club there and they have their own boathouse and a place where they can keep their things. A little property they rent cheaply. It was a small disused waterside inn which lost its licence. The ladies of the club can cook meals there and it's most convenient and delightful. I've often thought of joining but I seem to have so many other things to do in my spare time."

Littlejohn rose and shook hands with the manager, who repeated the arrangements for next day's visit.

"Thank you so much, sir, for your ready help. By the way, what did you say the name of the waterside inn was?"

"I don't remember mentioning the name, but it was a very appropriate one. *The Bargees' Rest*. It looks as if the club will soon have to buy the property from the executors. The owner was found drowned in the canal a little time ago. A man by the name of Plaster. . . ."

3

DEAD MAN'S COLLEAGUES

MOORGATE SEEMED BREATHLESS under the merciless heat of the sun and the air was hot and stagnant. It was a relief to Littlejohn to turn in at the Home Counties Bank, which was cool in contrast. The manager at once ordered coffee and pressed a switch which illuminated on the door a little sign, *Engaged*. Thereupon, Mr. Carr, the assistant manager, a young man eager for experience, took over the routine of the day.

Mr. Abbott looked more worried than ever.

" I've been thinking, Superintendent. . . . This isn't going to create any scandal, is it? "

" In what way, sir? "

" All this talk of teddy-boys and other irregularities has disturbed me."

" We'll handle it with discretion, sir. I've no doubt it will all soon blow over."

Mr. Abbott looked relieved. The word discretion comforted him.

" Where do you wish to begin, Littlejohn? "

He handed the Superintendent a cup of hot coffee.

" How many of a staff have you here, sir? "

" Fourteen, including myself. There are eight men and six girls."

" Are all the men members of the boating club? "

" Except me. Mr. Carr, my deputy, is nominally a member, but doesn't go much. He lives in Kent. Too far away. Of the remaining six, one, Myers, is accountant. Then there's Falconer, the chief cashier. Bastable was Falconer's deputy. Bastable's replacement is now on the way. Then there are one other cashier—he's indisposed—a senior clerk and a junior."

" Would it be any use my meeting some of the staff who were friends of Bastable? "

" Of course. Who would you like to see first? You'd better meet Carr, my assistant, I think."

He opened a communicating door between his room and the next and called-in Carr. Introductions.

"The Superintendent is here making enquiries about Bastable. It seems a teddy-boy who died the other night passed some comments about Bastable's suicide to a priest at the deathbed. The Superintendent is seeking more information."

Mr. Carr was about forty, a man of promise, favourably regarded by Head Office. He wore formal black jacket and striped grey trousers and was dark complexioned, with black hair held securely in place by brilliantine. He was a courteous, imperturbable man as a rule, but at the news just given, he looked alarmed.

"Teddy-boys! Ridiculous! Bastable would never have associated with such types."

Mr. Abbott looked nettled.

" It could hardly be ridiculous if it was the subject of a deathbed interview with a priest. . . ."

He'd been told to keep Mr. Carr in his place and, by gad, he would do so!

" I'm sorry, sir. But it seems so out of character."

Littlejohn took up the interview.

" We have records about Mr. Bastable's death, Mr. Carr, but could you tell me in your own words, exactly what happened? "

Carr looked embarrassed. He'd a very irritable customer in his room. In fact, he'd been surprised at Mr. Abbott interrupting the interview. The client might at any time explode and close his account!

" I think perhaps Mr. Falconer would be better than me for the purpose. He was the last to see Bastable alive. I'm just in the middle of an interview, too. . . ."

He turned to his chief and uttered one word.

" Gadsby."

"Oh God! You'd better leave us, then, Carr. We'll send for Falconer."

Carr made a courteous exit and could later be heard apologizing to the unseen occupant of his room.

Littlejohn was puzzled by the embarrassment of Carr. The look on his face when Bastable's name had been mentioned had not been a pleasant one at all.

"Didn't Carr and Bastable hit it off, Mr. Abbott?"

The manager removed his glasses and polished them briskly. There were dark rings of worry under his eyes.

"I can't say they did. Bastable used to complain that Carr was always needling him. Carr is very efficient and I can't say the same of poor Bastable. He used to regard himself as simply a cashier and didn't take to doing work other than on the counter. Now and then, when we're busy, some help on the accountant's department is always welcome. It gets the staff away at a reasonable hour. Carr thought Bastable could have found time to do a little more than he did. They quarrelled about it."

"Is that all, sir?"

Mr. Abbott looked surprised, almost scared. Surely, the police were not turning a case of suicide into one of murder by a colleague!

"All? Should there be more?"

"Perhaps not. If there *is* anything peculiar or strained about the relations of Bastable and any of his colleagues, though, I do depend on you to tell me, sir. This is not a superficial enquiry. I must say, sir, the teddy-boy seemed to have been blackmailing Bastable."

Mr. Abbott's hair almost stood on end.

"Blackmail! That's a nasty word. Whatever had Bastable been doing? I can't think. . . . But that doesn't involve any of his colleagues, does it?"

"It may do."

"I sincerely hope not. I do hope not."

Mr. Abbott, who was now smoking, absent-mindedly seized a piece of toast and bit it. Then he realized what he was doing and looked first at his cigarette and then at the stub of toast in his fingers and seemed surprised.

" Could we see Mr. Falconer, sir? "

" Of course."

Mr. Abbott pressed a button marked, *Cashier*. Nothing happened. Then he pressed it again and kept his finger on it. Somewhere in the office a buzzer could be heard.

A knock on the door and a man appeared.

" Is the buzzer out of order? "

" No, sir. I was just getting rid of a customer."

" Very well. This is Superintendent Littlejohn, Falconer. This is Mr. Falconer, our chief cashier."

More handshakes and a brief explanation about Bastable and the teddy-boy.

Falconer didn't seem a bit surprised. He looked a queer fish. A tall, loose-limbed man in his fifties, and almost completely bald. He had a pink, smooth face and a large flushed nose, obviously from alcohol. An air of familiarity, almost intimacy, and it was apparent he didn't feel much respect for Mr. Abbott, or for anybody else for that matter. He gave Littlejohn a sardonic smile.

" Poor old Bastable. I can't understand it. He was the last man. . . ."

" Yes, we know all that, Falconer. The Superintendent just wishes to ask you one or two questions about his death. He was your closest colleague and you were the last to see him alive."

The twinkle in Falconer's eye grew sad for a minute.

" Yes, that's true. If I'd stayed on another quarter of an hour, I might have prevented the tragedy. . . ."

There was resignation in the voice now.

" Please tell me exactly what happened on the night Bastable died, Mr. Falconer."

Falconer sat down and crossed his long legs. There was casualness about all he did. His words came out in a lazy drawl.

" I remember we'd balanced the cash and we'd been kept rather late, because we'd a heavy reserve and I decided to send some of it to headquarters next day. We were busy making it up. We put the lot away about five-thirty."

He took out a cigarette and lit it, although, judging from the manager's expression, he was breaking the rules. Then, he lolled back again, taking it easy.

"We locked the vault and I went home almost at once. I left Bastable downstairs, washing himself. The washroom's there as well as the strongroom."

"What about the keys, Mr. Falconer? I believe there is a security routine, a kind of ritual, connected with the holding of keys."

Falconer looked questioningly at Mr. Abbott, who nodded to indicate that he might carry on.

"The door of the cash vault has two keys and a combination lock. I, as chief cashier, carry one key and Mr. Carr, the assistant manager, carries the other. On the night Bastable died, however, Bastable was carrying Mr. Carr's key temporarily. . . ."

Abbott intervened.

"You see, Superintendent, Carr was down at Head Office discussing a large overdraft and it was arranged that Bastable should hold Carr's key, lock-up, and then call at Head Office on his way home and hand his key to Mr. Carr for the night. It was quite regular. When Carr is away on holidays or such, Bastable is relief-holder for his key and carries it till he returns."

Falconer nodded lazily.

"If Bastable hadn't arranged to call with the key at Head Office . . . it's just round the corner in Lothbury . . . he and I would have gone home together. We both live in Barnet and most nights we travel with one another. As it was, I left him and went off alone."

"You left about five-thirty?"

"Yes."

"The two of you were the last in the office?"

"That's right."

It was all said so casually. Falconer seemed quite unimaginative and the remembrance of his last night with his old friend apparently gave rise to no unpleasant thoughts. In fact he sounded a bit bored by it all.

"Now about the gun, sir. It was an old revolver which belonged to the bank, I believe."

"Yes. Years ago, there was an issue of revolvers. We used to have them handy in the tills. There'd been a number of raids at the time. After the first world war. They were eventually called-in and police-whistles were distributed instead. . . ."

Again the sardonic smile, the slow gesture of contempt. Whistles, indeed!

"And the one which Bastable used wasn't handed-in?"

"No. I don't know why. There was an old branch on this site before the new one was built. It was brought from there in a cash-box full of odds and ends . . . old coins, out-of-date cheque forms. . . . The kind of junk that accumulates. . . ."

He said it sadly as though he himself might have been included in the old junk which accumulated, too.

"It was so out-of-date that the metal part was of brass."

"Yes. I've seen it, sir, among the exhibits which I had brought-in to Scotland Yard. It was a bit defective, too."

"That's right. I think that might have been the reason for it not being surrendered when they were called-in. The hammer was a bit wonky and went off very easily. As a matter of fact, I believe in the old office they were fooling about with it once, and it fired. There were a few cartridges left and they must have been loading it. They used to show the hole where the bullet went in the upholstered seat of a stool. It ricochetted round the office. Luckily nobody was hurt . . . I was told, the manager was out at lunch whilst they were larking."

Mr. Abbott didn't think that was funny at all. He was getting bored by Falconer's presence and irritated by his insolent manner.

"Was the gun ever brought out in recent times?"

"No. Now and then, when we tidied-up, we'd look at it as a curio, you know. It just stayed in the rubbish-box."

"Loaded?"

"No. The cartridges were there with it."

Mr. Abbott was rattled by the very mention of the gun.

"I never knew of its presence there. It was highly irregular to keep it at all. It ought to have been turned-in or else broken-up and thrown away."

"I suppose it ought."

"Bastable knew about it?"

"Yes. But I'd no idea he'd taken it from the box before we locked-up. He must have slipped it in his pocket as he was putting his cash away. After I left, he used it, I'm afraid."

"How had Bastable behaved just before he died? Did he seem depressed or worried?"

"Yes. He'd been a bit vacant all the week. I asked him was anything the matter. We were friends, you know, and I thought I might be able to help him. He said there was nothing wrong. He'd just been a bit off colour. Something he'd eaten, perhaps."

"Did you have any idea what might have caused his mood?"

"Well. . . ."

He looked at Abbott in an easy, familiar kind of way, as though they might have been equals in the service.

"Well, Falconer? You might as well tell the Superintendent what's on your mind. You've already discussed it with the rest of the office."

Falconer nodded agreement.

"Yes. His cash was wrong, it turned out later. And he hadn't a ghost of a chance of putting it right, in my view. He was broke."

"How do you know?"

"We were paid salaries on June 18th. Bastable died on the 23rd. It's no secret that he drew all but ten pounds of his salary in cash the day he got it. Presumably to pay his debts. He'd ten pounds left to see him through four or five weeks. He was in a hopeless financial mess."

"Why? Was he gambling or speculating?"

"I don't think so. He never gave the slightest hint of it. No; his wife was extravagant and spent every cent he'd give her. She's just one of ... well ... those kind of women. ..."

Abbott looked uneasy and had grown hot with embarrassment.

" I don't think you need to discuss Mrs. Bastable any more, Falconer. She's taken all this very badly and is in great trouble."

Another sardonic smile, almost impudent in its implications.

" Very well, sir. You asked me to be candid about things. Will there be anything more, Superintendent? It's nearly lunch-time and the counter will be getting short of staff."

" Just one more question, Mr. Falconer. Did you know a man named Plaster? "

Falconer had risen to his feet ready to go and now was lolling with his hands on the back of his chair.

" Yes."

The voice was quite natural, almost pleasant. As though he were glad to remember the name.

" I don't know whether you've heard or not, but he was found drowned in the canal some time ago. He was a hopeless drunkard and it was thought he'd taken too much and walked in. I knew him through the dramatic society and our canal boating club."

" How was he connected with them? "

" He was a furniture dealer in South Mimms. I'm a member of a dramatic group at Barnet. . . . So was Bastable. . . . Quite a few of our staff are. I'm not an actor myself, but my wife takes leading parts sometimes. . . ."

With his flushed large nose, his bald head and his blank, almost desolate look, he might easily have made-up as harlequin or a clown. His bored voice continued.

" Plaster used to be good at scene-painting and did quite a lot for us. We first contacted him about borrowing furniture for our shows. He'd all kinds of period and other stuff, useful for the job. He was always about the place when we were putting-on a play. Then, he bought an old pub on the canal bank, which lost its licence and shut up when there wasn't enough traffic on the water to support it. He rented it to us. We were interested in sailing on the canal. We formed a club in summer among the play-group to keep us together when the acting season was over. We did the old pub up and made a club of it and a boathouse. We called it *The Bargees' Rest*. Now, with Plaster dead, I guess we'll have to buy it, if the price is right."

" It sounds very interesting. Will you take me there one evening, soon? "

Falconer still didn't seem surprised. Nothing surprised him. In fact, his face showed faint signs of pleasure.

" Of course. Any time. Just 'phone me and we'll go out together. We've bought a stove there and the women do a bit of cooking. My wife'll make us a meal. Let me know."

He shook hands with Littlejohn as he left. Steady, useful hands he possessed, too.

Mr. Abbott gave a sigh of relief.

" Rather a queer fish, sir," said Littlejohn.

" I agree with you. He's a very good cashier and never wrong in his cash. But that's all. He's fifty-five and not long off retirement. What he'll do with himself then, I don't know. He seems at a loose end now."

" He's not gone very far in your service, sir."

" It's his own fault. He's got brains if he'll use them. And, as you see, he's a cool customer and well able to look after himself. But his whole record is one of lackadaisical, lazy drifting. He could have made a career if he'd taken the trouble. He's been offered quite a number of promising jobs. But when he went to Head Office for interview, he didn't seem to care. No ambition . . . a drifter. . . ."

" Will it be convenient for me to see Mr. Myers, the accountant? I believe he was a friend of Bastable, too."

" Yes. They lived near one another and Myers is one of the acting-boating gang as well. I'll ring for him."

Myers was a different type altogether. He knocked on the manager's door, entered sturdily and purposively, and waited for his instructions.

" Come in, Myers. Sit down. This is Superintendent Little-john, of Scotland Yard. . . ."

The same rigmarole again. The teddy-boy, Bastable, the death-bed scene. Myers listened quietly, ready to help if he could.

He was tall and heavily built, exuding energy from every pore. The kind who would row his boat and even take a swim in the canal every morning before breakfast if he felt like it. A bit plebeian and coarse-grained, too, and he didn't choose his clothes and ties like Falconer. He was without waistcoat and the white shirt which covered his beefy chest had his initials embroidered in blue over his heart. FJM.

Myers said he'd gone home when Falconer and Bastable were in the basement putting away the cash. His wife had invited friends to a meal at a little club they frequented and he wanted to be there as soon as he could.

" *The Bargees' Rest*, sir? "

Myers raised his eyebrows.

" Yes. Do you know the place? "

" We've just been talking to Mr. Falconer about it. And about the late Mr. Plaster, as well."

" Oh, Plaster. A sticky end, wasn't it? Walked into the canal when he was dead-drunk."

So, they all thought that. Nobody suspected Bastable of chucking him in and leaving him to drown.

" Do you serve drink at the club? "

" We've no licence, but we keep our own supplies in the lockers. It belongs, really, to the locker-holder, but we share and share alike, you know."

" Did Bastable strike you as being worried just before he died, Mr. Myers? "

" He was always worried. If it wasn't nervousness about his cash, over which he was a great fusser, it was something else. He seemed to have a job to make ends meet, too. He was always hard-up. His wife . . ."

Mr. Abbott intervened again.

" I don't think it's right to discuss his widow in the present circumstances. After all, it would only be gossip, wouldn't it, to talk about the Bastables' personal relations . . . ? "

The manager was flushed. Myers looked put-out.

" I really didn't think. . . ."

" That's all right, Myers. Have you anything more to tell the Superintendent about Bastable? "

Littlejohn wondered why Abbott seemed so eager to protect the dead man's wife. After all, the two men, Myers and Falconer, had been polite enough about her. A spendthrift, that was all. He wondered if Abbott feared something else might come out.

The photographs of Bastable, taken for the inquest, had been produced for Littlejohn. A medium-built, slender man, fair haired, thin faced, weak featured. . . . Nondescript. The kind of man you'd pass in the street and never even notice. Even in a police photograph, he'd somehow given you the impression that he'd nobody to look after him, to take good care of him. Negative and neglected, that was it.

And now, they were saying, when Abbott would allow them, that his wife was extravagant.

" What kind of a man *was* Bastable? "

Both Abbott and Myers looked uneasy. As though Littlejohn had asked them to disclose the confidential secrets of the bank.

" Perhaps Myers had better give you his views."

Mr. Abbott was cautious and probably preferred to speak after the accountant had left them.

" He was a very decent fellow. My wife and I had quite a lot to do with him and his wife. We live at South Mimms and he and his wife at Barnet. He was born in that part. Falconer lived in Barnet, too, but he came from Yorkshire several years ago and we and the Bastables took him under our wing, and he and his wife eventually found a house near us. That's how it is we're all interested in dramatic work and canal sailing together. We formed a little gang and gradually it grew to be a sort of club. They're not all bank people. . . ."

Myers looked lost in his discourse.

" I was telling you about Bastable. . . . I must be frank and say that he wasn't much use in a bank. Cashiering was about as far as he'd go. He was careful enough, because he was naturally fussy and nervous. A man like that's no use in the main office. If you're nervous and fussy you delay the work and infect other people with lack of confidence. It holds up everything. That's why he got stuck here on the counter. There was nothing to which to promote him. He was a stick-in-the-mud. Once, when Head Office wanted to move him, he kicked up such a fuss that they said he'd better stay where he was. Didn't they, sir?"

Abbott nodded concurrence.

"He was quiet, good mannered, polite to customers, who all liked him. But he'd a . . . a . . . you could almost call it a sad way with him. Apologetic. Defeated. . . . That's the word. Defeated. You'd think that sometime in the past he'd made a big mistake and had suffered for it. Like a dog with its spirit broken after ill-treatment."

Mr. Abbott squirmed.

"Come, come, Myers. This isn't the dramatic society. Let's say he lacked any energy and initiative."

"That's right, sir."

"He'd no children?"

"No, sir. He bred dogs at one time and then started to keep rabbits, but it all petered out. His wife . . ."

He halted. That was taboo.

All the same, Littlejohn was now sure he'd better see Mrs. Bastable as soon as possible. Her name kept cropping-up, only to be vetoed by Abbott. The other men wanted to talk about her and her extravagance. . . . Somehow she was connected with the rabbits and the dogs, which had fallen through, too! And she'd had hysterics when Bastable shot himself and had gone to live with her mother now, far enough away.

"Will there be anything more, sir?"

Myers was eager to get away. Probably his lunch was in the offing.

"Has Mr. Falconer any children?"

"No."

"And you . . . ?"

Myers looked like a family man. He'd probably half-a-dozen.

"Three, sir. A girl of ten and two boys, seven and five. We call them the Water Babies down at *The Bargees' Rest.* . . ."

Mr. Abbott was getting restive.

"It's past lunch time, Mr. Myers, and if the Superintendent doesn't need you any more. . . ."

"No, sir. Very many thanks, Mr. Myers. We'll meet again. Mr. Falconer's invited me down to *The Bargees' Rest.*"

"Good! Good! You'll meet my wife and the Water Babies there, then. Looking forward to seeing you. . . ."

Mr. Abbott was fatigued. After all, a thorough enquiry into Bastable's death and a sort of family-coach among the officials didn't occur every day. It was a strain.

"Would you care to have lunch with me, Littlejohn? We can talk more then."

"I'm sorry, sir. I must get back to the Yard. We're short-handed. Besides, I've taken too much of your time already. . . ."

"Not at all. Come again any time, if I can help."

"Thank you. Do you think any other members of your staff could give me useful background about Bastable? Was he friendly with any of the rest?"

"I don't think so. The third cashier has only been here a month. He hardly knew Bastable. The other clerk, Vance, and the junior are, of course, interested in the canal club. Edgell, the junior, who lives in Putney, scutters off there regularly on his motor-bike and Vance has a car he uses. He lives in Ealing. You could speak to them if you like."

"I'll leave it until later. I don't wish to take up a lot of the staff's time. It isn't fair. What about the lady members?"

"One is on the counter; the rest are on machines and routine. I'd hardly call Bastable a ladies' man, Littlejohn. As I said, there are six girls. Miss Browning is the senior. She's about twenty-five and is a cashier. The rest are around twenty; some of them younger. I don't think they'd have much that's useful to tell you. You might like to talk with Miss Browning. She's a sensible girl."

"Next time I call, then, sir."

They said good-bye and Abbott took Littlejohn to the door.

"If you think of anything more in which I can help, please don't hesitate to come again."

He got the impression that Abbott was uneasy about something, but couldn't lay his finger on it. He stood at the edge of the kerb lighting his pipe and as he did so, two younger clerks left the bank, stared hard at him, and then crossed the road and entered a café. Probably Edgell and Vance. He'd leave them to Cromwell later.

When Littlejohn arrived back at Scotland Yard, he found that his instructions to question the teddy-boys, who'd been brought in after the Lambeth scuffle and had been before the magistrate that morning, had been carried out. They both swore that nobody had been after Alfie Batt on the night of the fight. It had just been an ordinary fight against intruders in their territory. Alfie had merely climbed the roof to cheat the police.

"Christine always has to make everything sound like it was on the flicks. Too much imagination. That's what's wrong with Christine."

And they paid their fines and went home to fight another day.

4

QUARTETTE AT *THE RAVEN*

" MIND IF I sit here? "

The place was packed and there was some excuse for Cromwell's polite intrusion.

Vance and Egdell looked up at the tall, powerful stranger, holding his bowler hat almost ceremonially over his heart, and smiled. He wore a dark suit of heavy serge, waistcoat and all, and the very sight of him at eighty in the shade, made them sweat from every pore.

" Of course. . . ."

Cromwell hung-up his hat on a row of hooks on the wall. It was full to capacity already, but, with an experienced eye, he sought out another bowler smaller than his own, and crowned it. The noise of conversation in the long, crowded restaurant was deafening.

The Raven was popular. Cromwell, following Littlejohn's instructions, had waited in the street for the two bank clerks and followed them in. He was supposed to chat informally over lunch. But he was almost disappointed. The two occupied places at a table for four were only just vacated in time. Which left them with a seat to spare.

Vance kept a watchful eye on the head of the stairs, for they were on the first floor. Cromwell had hardly seated himself on the little chair at the tightly fitting table, when a good-looking, fair-haired girl appeared. Vance waved furiously—too furiously for normal interest—and the girl saw them. Vance forgot the menu and the stranger, and rose and helped her to her seat. He signalled to the waitress half-a-dozen times until the harassed girl came and rebuked him.

" I can't be everywhere at once. . . ."

The newcomer wrinkled her nose at the idea of soup.

Whereat, Vance did some arguing to substitute tomato-juice. The waitress finally gave in.

"I ought to charge you extra, but seein' that it's you. . . ."

"Same for me," said Cromwell.

The waitress looked hard at him. He wasn't a regular, and not entitled to favours.

"Are you with them?"

"Yes."

They all smiled and it broke the ice.

Then, the three in the party ordered chicken and trifle. Cromwell did the same. Vance kept calling the girl Barbara.

"You'll be able to come to the canal tonight?"

It sounded like another Plaster tragedy cooking-up!

"Ted rang and asked me to play tennis at the club."

The old game. Cat and mouse. Poor Vance was head over heels in love and the girl knew it. Cromwell, who prided himself on an illusion that he knew all about feminine psychology—in fact, another Stendhal, whose book on *L'Amour* he'd read in a pocket-edition translation—almost tapped Vance on the shoulder and told him to tell her to go with Ted, then, and that he couldn't care less. . . . Instead. . . .

"What, again! Besides, it's too hot for tennis. The water's cool and romantic these evenings on the canal. . . ."

The canal, indeed!

"I may come. I'll see what the weather's like and how I feel when we finish. Besides, we're being rude to Walter."

Young Edgell, still a boy, in spite of his fancy tie, his spreading collar and his draped jacket, blushed to the roots of his crew-cut.

"That's all right, Miss Browning. I don't mind at all."

So, all three of them were from the bank. Cromwell almost rubbed his hands. Good! He wouldn't be embarrassed by a lot of love-making whilst he got his information. There's nothing bank clerks like talking about more than the bank, a chartered accountant he'd once arrested had told him.

Cromwell thought he'd got all three of them sized-up

already. Edgell, the junior, honoured by dining with older colleagues. Cromwell was wrong there. He did it because the place was cheap and he was sweet on Vance's younger sister, Marlene—a smasher, in his opinion—and wanted him to invite him home.

Vance, deduced Cromwell, with his keenness on the canal, his tall, well-built body, rugged healthy face, and his easy and rather shabby style of dress, was obviously a sportsman and keen on the open-air. Wrong again! Vance was nothing of the kind. He played billiards and bowls well and his shabbiness was due to trying to save-up on a limited salary. He was twenty-eight and determined to marry Miss Browning, Ted or no Ted. So, he had joined the gang at *The Bargees' Rest*, of which she had been a regular member till Vance turned-up. She wasn't as cruel as Cromwell decided. Although he didn't know it, Vance had landed her! But she had to cool him down. Let news of their mutual affection reach Mr. Abbott, and one of them would be moved to another branch! Two participants in the same love's young dream are a bit too much in the severe precincts of one bank office.

" May I ask if you all work in the Home Counties branch opposite? " said Cromwell between the tomato-juice and the chicken.

" May I also ask why you wish to know? "

Vance said it sharply. He scented a spy fishing for information for a raid. Vance was naturally courteous. His face was humorous and his dark eyes had a pleasant twinkle. But he was determined to show Miss Browning that he could handle the situation.

" I'm from the police. If you'd care to see my warrant-card . . . ? I knew you two gentlemen came from over the way and I hoped to have a word with you. It's easier, isn't it, than doing it formally in the office under the manager's eye? "

" You're telling me. "

Chicken, blue-looking canned peas, and chips then appeared over their shoulders. Cromwell wondered where all the legs of chicken came from and what had happened to the rest of the birds.

Cromwell's smile and solemn cheerful manner made them all at ease.

" Nice fellow. . . . A bit shy. Hell of an appetite, though," Vance later told his pals.

Cromwell recited the tale again. The curtain-raiser about the teddy-boy and Bastable and the confession at the hospital to Father Silvester, but no mention of Plaster's death.

" It's made us need to look closer into Bastable's death. The coroner might have been mistaken about suicide. Suppose this teddy-boy. . . ."

And he left them to imagine the rest.

" You mean it might have been murder? "

Edgell's eyes shot half out of their sockets. He'd now given up the unequal struggle with his chicken limbs and was dealing with the chips and peas as politely as he could.

" We've got to be satisfied, you'll agree."

" We do."

Vance said it with such determination and sincerity, that Miss Browning cast upon him a look of admiration which, had he seen it, would have made him forget crime and Bastable entirely.

" So I just came along for an informal little chat about the bank staff and Bastable. I'm glad we've met. It makes things easier, doesn't it? "

They all agreed it did.

" Is there anything particular you want to know, sir? "

Vance had become the spokesman, although the girl was obviously itching to talk as soon as she could get a chance. All three, however, manifested the peculiar, habitual banking caution, conjured by a convention as solemn as the Hippocratic Oath itself. If it came to discussing business they were all going to be sticky.

A hand cumbrously moved the dirty plates.

" Isn't the chicken good? " asked an offended voice from the rear.

" Yes, Jessie, but we're too hot to dismember it."

Jessie didn't know what Vance was talking about, but she thought he was a proper caution.

"What about ice-cream instead of trifle? We've got some for specials."

Four ice-creams.

Littlejohn had shown Cromwell his notes on the interviews of the previous day.

"Bastable had a good-looking wife, hadn't he?" began the sergeant enthusiastically.

The trio from the bank were disappointed. Here they were, expecting some kind of police third-degree and all the man was interested in was Irma! They were fed-up with Irma. Especially Miss Browning. She remembered the last bank dance. The low-cut gown and the men almost fighting for dances with Irma. Disgusting! And poor old Bastable smiling his beaten smile and pretending he hadn't noticed.

"If you like them that way," said Vance.

Barbara decided she'd go to the canal after all!

"Extravagant?"

"Yes," said Miss Browning. "That low-cut dance frock must have cost twenty-five guineas, at least. Irma wasn't the kind who'd buy one at the sales."

"Made Bastable a bit hard-up?"

"A bit? Don't you know that he was a thousand light in his cash-balance when he died?"

"Yes. I'm coming to that. So, he might have got to the end of his tether about being broke. His wife's extravagances, her neglect of him. . . ."

The three from the bank exchanged glances.

"And other things. She couldn't leave the men alone."

Miss Browning thought it time for plain speaking.

"Rushing round the shops and having affairs with men. . . ."

Vance was worried. He felt like telling Barbara not to exaggerate. On the other hand, the situation between them was a bit tricky and delicately balanced. He decided to keep quiet.

"What men?" asked Cromwell.

"At the dramatic society. . . . Even at the canal. The way she used to dress at the canal! Half-naked and always getting bitten by insects and needing first-aid from the men."

Miss Browning was an expert witness. She even remembered Irma and Vance . . . yes, Vance . . . and the bottle of iodine. Her thoughts turned briefly to Ted again, who thought of nothing but improving his service at tennis.

Four ices, almost liquid, arrived. That brought the discussion back to earth.

"Four coffees . . . on me," said Cromwell, deciding that his expenses account would stand it. "Was anybody in particular mixed-up with Mrs. Bastable of late?"

"Carr, our Assistant-Manager, made a bit of a fool of himself at the last dance in February. He's a bachelor and has an eye for the ladies. He's a good dancer, and so is Irma. They couldn't keep them apart that night. Cheek to cheek! They seemed to dance like one person. It was just disgusting! "

Everything about Irma seemed disgusting to Miss Browning!

"Even Abbott, our manager, was a bit soft on her. Not that he'd misbehave himself. He's too decent for that. But you know how fatherly and protective some middle-aged men get over a good-looking woman. . . ."

Cromwell did. It was in Littlejohn's notes. "Mr. Abbott seemed anxious to defend Bastable's wife from any responsibility for his death."

It was all coming out. Cromwell was pleased. In his movements of satisfaction he knocked his ice-cream dish from the table and smashed it. This resulted in an unusual immediate arrival of the waitress who told him it would have to go on his bill.

"What kind of woman is Irma? Her appearance, I mean."

Vance hesitated diplomatically, but Miss Browning, who read modern fiction, quickly drew the picture.

"She was younger than Bastable by quite a bit. I don't know how she ever came to marry him. It's said she was once on the stage. I doubt it. The producer of our dramatic society at Barnet, however, seemed to believe it, or else she charmed him into giving her good parts. She was always the *femme fatale*. She didn't need to act it, I can tell you. She just had to be herself. When it came to real acting . . . well . . . She was just a ham."

Coffee. It tasted like acorns, but it kept their heads together. It was 1.45, too. The bank trio were due back at 2.0.

". . . She's a full-bodied woman of forty, dark and striking, with challenging eyes and sensual lips. . . ."

Vance's coffee went down the wrong way and he choked with coughing. He'd never thought Barbara had it in her! She hadn't really. She'd remembered it from an American crime tale she was reading. But how was Vance to know? He thought it was original.

"Myers is a family man, I believe."

It sounded flat and banal after Irma.

"Yes. A very nice chap. Nothing between him and Irma, I can assure you. He's a one-woman man, if you know what I mean. Eyes only for his wife."

Vance said the end of it in italics for Miss Browning's benefit. He was the same . . . he hoped.

"And Falconer?"

"You seem to know everybody."

"It's our business, Mr. Vance. Besides, my chief took a list from Mr. Abbott, when he called at the bank yesterday."

"Are *we* on it?"

"You're all on it, Miss Browning. But Superintendent Littlejohn didn't have the pleasure of meeting you three yesterday. He missed seeing three very nice people, if you'll allow me to say so."

They all looked as though they'd allow him, and smiled. Vance was particularly pleased. A testimonial in the hearing of Barbara! His heart warmed to Cromwell.

"We'll do all we can to help you. You were saying . . . Falconer? He's a good cashier, but beyond that, he's dead from the neck upwards. No ambition, no push. . . . Too fond of the bottle. . . ."

Miss Browning, as Cromwell, feminine psychologist, expected, had to put Vance right.

"But a perfect gentleman. I feel a bit sorry for him. He's been very well educated."

"I give you that, Barbara. A gentleman. Well bred. But gone to seed. Am I right?"

No reply.

"Why are you sorry for him, Miss Browning?"

"I think perhaps his wife hasn't been much help to him. Oh, she's a lovely woman. But she's a bit of a doll. Brown hair, blue eyes, milk-and-roses complexion, tall. . . . And yet she's insipid. That's right, isn't it, Peter?"

Vance agreed eagerly.

"They're unsuited?"

"I don't know, Mr. Cromwell. I really don't. They're always impeccably polite to each other and Falconer is most attentive to her. He waits on her hand and foot and she keeps him at it, too. And yet . . . they somehow seem bored stiff with each other. I'm sure that's Falconer's reason for drinking so much. He's just bored with Fleur and her budgerigars and her poodles. . . ."

"Any children?"

"No. Alec—that's Falconer—is always so nice to her. Irma couldn't break his imperturbability. He's one of her failures."

"She's tried?"

"She's tried everybody."

"Was Falconer in the war?"

"Yes. He was a bit of a hero, I gather. He speaks French well . . . or did. He was parachuted into France a time or two on special missions. You wouldn't think so now, would you?"

"I'm afraid I've not met him, Miss Browning."

Cromwell looked at the clock again. Two o'clock. He remembered that Littlejohn had gone to Brighton to see Irma. He'd just be there now. He wondered what kind of a reception the Superintendent would get!

"Well. It's time I left you to return to duty."

There was a committee meeting.

"If you could tell Mr. Abbott, if he turns nasty, that we're late back because you've been questioning us, we might get away with another fifteen minutes."

"Thanks. I'll be brief. There's not much more. How many of you are there in the boating-club on the canal?"

"Oh, there are about a hundred and twenty members. We need all their subs to keep the place going. But we tend to break-up into cliques, you know. Ours has about twenty in it. Mostly our staff and their wives and sweethearts. . . ."

Vance gave Barbara a significant look as he said it. She replied with a cold defensive stare.

"One or two of the party aren't in the bank. It might be a good idea if you came down one evening, incog., Mr. Cromwell. I'd introduce you as a friend of mine interested in boating. . . . You could meet the gang. It would perhaps be helpful."

"Thanks. I'll have to see about it. We're short-handed at the Yard at present, though. Holidays. . . ."

He remembered that Littlejohn had talked of going down to *The Bargees' Rest* himself. The Superintendent would be more at home than he on such a job. Cromwell thought of himself in a yachting-cap, rowing a boat up and down the canal in this hot weather. And perhaps Irma, half-naked, being stung by mosquitoes. . . .

"Are they all members of the dramatic society, as well?"

"Oh, no. Most of the playing-members of the acting group have joined. It's a good idea to keep them together in the summer while the plays are on ice, you see."

"Has Mrs. Bastable been seen since her husband died?"

Miss Browning's chance.

"Has she been? Rather. The distressed widow seeking comfort. It's a wonder she didn't come down in a black veil. All the men were stricken, of course, and heaped consolations upon her. . . ."

The time was up.

"Did any of you know a man called Plaster?"

They all knew him.

" A scene-painter, who also hired properties to the dramatic society. He was found drowned in the canal. Fell in when he was drunk. He was a proper soak."

" Did he frequent *The Bargees' Rest*? "

Vance nodded.

" He owned it. He was always there. Not our type at all, you know. A bit of a bounder . . . a twister, if you ask me. I wouldn't be surprised if he'd turned out to be receiving stolen goods, on the side. I heard he did moneylending, too, now and then. A fellow down at the club told me Plaster had offered to lend him the money to buy a car. He'd been complaining about not being able to afford one, so Plaster dropped a hint."

" Any of your men involved? "

" Oh dear no. It's against the rules to deal with money-lenders. It would mean the sack if word got out."

They were already on the way out.

" All the same. . . ."

Young Edgell found his tongue for the first time.

" Yes? "

" Bastable might have been in Plaster's clutches, you know. I never thought Plaster was a moneylender. I always thought he was a bookie in a small way. Just before Plaster died . . . a week or so . . . I saw Bastable giving him some pound notes one night at *The Bargees' Rest*. Plaster seemed mad with Bastable about something at the time. Told him if he didn't pay-up there'd be trouble. He'd either sue him or report it to the bank."

Vance looked surprised.

" How did you hear all this? "

" I'd gone in the club for a drink. I was standing by the window that overlooks the back. The pair of them were on their own and I could hear Plaster shouting and Bastable telling him to keep his voice down, everybody would hear them."

" What did Bastable say? "

" He gave him some bank-notes, which Plaster pushed away at first. Then he snatched them and put them in his

pocket. Bastable said he'd get the rest by the week-end and
Plaster said he'd better, or else it would be worse for him.
Bastable lost his temper a bit. I've never seen him in a rage
before. He was usually quiet when he was in trouble. In
fact, he'd a whining way with him. I've even seen him in
tears when his luck's been out. But this time, he went off
the deep end. He called Plaster a bloodsucker and blackmailer."

" What did Plaster say to that? "

" He just laughed. He said something about Bastable
would know where to get it. ' Same old place,' he said, very
offensively, I thought. He must have meant Bastable could
dip his hand in the till."

Vance was making distress signals.

" It's half-past. There'll be hell to pay. Don't forget, Mr.
Cromwell, if he rings-up Scotland Yard, you'll stand by our
story."

" I'll promise you that. Like me to come to see him now? "

" No thanks. We'll manage. . . ."

They shook hands all round.

" Remember, Mr. Cromwell, any time you like to make a
date with me to go to *The Bargees' Rest*, I'm at your dis-
posal. . . ."

Cromwell made his way happily down Moorgate in search
of his bus. He whistled his favourite tune to himself. " When
you and I were young, Maggie."

It hadn't been a bad interview at all.

5

IRMA

WHEN LITTLEJOHN GOT out of the train at Brighton, the air hit him like a hot blast. There wasn't even a sea-breeze. The faint aromas of frying and of grilled chops hung heavily on the atmosphere and people seemed to float lazily in it like a lot of fishes. It was the effect of the sun, merciless here as in London. The glare of it dimmed his vision and the heat penetrated to the very marrow of his bones.

A lot of people wandering about with next-to-nothing on, gramophones playing tunes to which they were too hot to dance. Everybody struggling to the shady sides of the streets, like exhausted swimmers making for a raft.

Twenty-six Chisholm Street, at right-angles to the promenade. Littlejohn had obtained the name of Irma Bastable's mother from the directory; Irma had left her address in the records.

Mrs. Louise (Lulu) Utting, aged sixty, furnished rooms. That was on the files of the Brighton police. She'd been in their hands for something and nothing. Getting her chimney on fire. Fined 10s. She was on the telephone and Littlejohn had rung her and arranged to see her and her daughter at two o'clock.

The house was a Georgian relic with a narrow front and a door which would have been more attractive for a coat of paint. He pulled the brass handle of the door-bell. There was a rattle of wires and nothing else. So he beat on the knocker.

At the far end of the pavement, he could see the promenade. Boats gliding idly on the sea; people in light suits, bathing costumes, and beach pyjamas milling about; extravagant cars and taxis whizzing past. Right at the end of the street, a man frenziedly cranking-up a car which had broken down.

Mrs. Utting opened the door. Littlejohn felt relieved right away. He knew her kind. You could see at once that she'd been connected with the stage at some time or other in her life.

A plump woman, she still bleached her hair and had a copious bosom. A small mouth with full lips, and, once upon a time, she'd had a good figure. Now, she'd run to seed a bit. All the same, she had a good-humoured look and, in her heyday, probably a saucy eye.

"Good afternoon. We're expecting you."

He got a hearty welcome, at least. As he followed her indoors, a ginger-headed, bony young man cannoned into them.

"Excuse me," and he was off. A boarder late for work.

The lobby was so dark that Littlejohn, still sun-blind, couldn't make out what was in it. A staircase straight ahead; the kitchen behind; and two more doors to a dining-room and a sitting-room—probably called the lounge. There was a smell of boiled beef and carrots hanging about.

"Come in the lounge."

He'd been right!

It wasn't a bad place. Little plastic-topped tables with ash-trays advertising beer. Cheap easy chairs, a worn carpet, some awful pictures on the walls, and a gas-fire with one element removed to prevent the lodgers lighting it.

"Sit down and make yourself comfortable. . . ."

She offered him a cigarette. She never stopped smoking. One after another. . . .

Hanging over the fireplace and standing on the mantel-piece were framed photographs of young women in tights or the ugly dresses of the twenties. Obviously all on the stage. Affectionate autographs scribbled all over them. "To Lulu, with love."

Lulu, according to the Brighton police, who seemed to know a lot about her, had started as a chorus-girl. Then, one night, a cabbie, who had been in the habit of giving her occasional lifts home, had seduced her. Irma had been the result. The cabby had, to his credit, almost at once married Lulu and right away taken to drink. He had finally fallen in the fire and left her a widow. Then she had become a dresser at a music-hall, until she'd become redundant. She'd been a thrifty sort and been able to set-up a small apartment house. This was it.

The record was unusually full. The policeman on the beat—himself a widower—had fancied hanging up his hat at Chisholm Street and making Mrs. Utting his number two. They had confided many things to each other, until a woman more enterprising had carried the bobby off.

From the start, Mrs. Utting showed great respect for the police, in spite of her broken romance. She never bore a grudge for long.

"You'll have to excuse my daughter, sir, being late. Her bereavement has upset her and she's not the girl she was. It's slowed her down. She'll be here in a minute or two."

A series of bumps and footsteps in the best front-room up above indicated that Irma was preparing for her entrance.

Mrs. Utting and Littlejohn were sitting opposite each other, smoking cigarettes, on each side of the woolly hearth-rug, as though they were lifelong friends.

"How is your daughter, Mrs. Utting?"

The woman sighed conventionally, but lost none of her good spirits.

"It was a terrible shock at first. She's much better now, but it'll take time for her to get over it properly. It was so unexpected."

A decent sort, and now quite at her ease. She didn't wish to rub the police the wrong way. Besides, the Superintendent was a nicely spoken man and knew his manners. Mrs. Utting felt at home with him.

"Your daughter was on the stage like yourself, Mrs. Utting?"

"Yes. She'd quite a promising career in front of her. It's in the blood, I suppose. I was on the halls myself till I got married. I encouraged Irma to go in for straight acting,

though. Life's not as rough in the proper theatre. But her
voice gave out. I spent a fortune on it, but it was no good.
She was resting with me here when she met Cyril Bastable."

"Was he on holiday?"

"Bless you, no! He was a regular. He was at the Brighton
branch of the bank at the time."

"And they fell for each other?"

"He was mad about her from the start and I think with
her being run-down in health, she let him persuade her. I
was surprised, I'll tell you. She could have done far better
than him. He hadn't started to go bald then, although he
was over ten years older than my girl, and was more pushing
then than later in life. At least, I mean, he was pushing about
Irma. He never left her alone. To tell the truth, I never
thought much of him. No *go* in him. I heard he was the
same at work."

She sat upright in her chair, her knees together. She was
showing Littlejohn that she knew how to behave like a lady.

"He was in a good, steady job, though, which is something. I know what it is to wonder where your next shilling
is coming from. But, as I said, Irma could have done better
. . . far better."

"You said you didn't expect anything like suicide. Bastable wasn't a melancholy man?"

"Not him. He wasn't temperamental enough for that. I
know what temperament is, I can tell you. My late husband
was temperamental. Cyril didn't have a scrap of it in him.
He was quiet, with no imagination. You should have seen
him when he fell for Irma. He was like a spaniel dog. He
worshipped the ground she trod on, always did. It's not the
way to treat a woman, you know, Superintendent. Irma
thought no better of him for it. . . ."

Littlejohn smiled.

"You can smile, if you like, but you're a man of the
world, Superintendent. You know as well as I do, that
women don't respect the men they can wipe their feet on.
That was the trouble between Cyril and Irma. He was too
soft with her."

She sat thinking about it placidly. Then, she sighed again.

"She was too good for Cyril, though I say it myself. Irma had intelligence, good looks and style when she married him . . . still has. . . ."

It was just growing interesting when footsteps began to descend the stairs. The door opened, and there was Irma. The *femme fatale*! Mrs. Utting said the bereavement had slowed her down. Littlejohn wondered what she was like when full-speed ahead!

She was certainly all they'd said about her and she entered with a gust of exotic perfume. It was probably good and expensive, but it was overdone. In no time, the room was reeking with it.

She was of medium build, with shapely arms and a luscious figure. A *retroussé* nose and full sensual lips. Almost jet-black hair trimmed rather short, a chubby face, and large, fine dark eyes. Her dark dress was deliberately *risqué*, and showed a lot of firm, white flesh. The fact that she had just become a widow had not damped her sparkle and freshness. She was beautiful, with a vulgar animal beauty.

But it was Irma's tremendous vitality which you noticed first. She radiated it. Poor Cyril Bastable must have been speechless and powerless against it, especially if she'd combined with it the voluptuous languor of an invalid when he first met her. He'd be in the web right away.

And Mrs. Utting had tried to make out that Cyril had swept Irma from her feet by his sheer fidelity! It was comic!

Mrs. Utting introduced them. Irma gave Littlejohn a warm firm handclasp, holding his hand a little longer than was called-for. Her eyes shone with what might have been tears or sheer coquetry as she thanked him for his sympathy.

He told them about the teddy-boy, but made no mention of the death of Plaster.

"I can't understand how Cyril came to be mixed-up with such a person. But then there's nothing about the whole affair that I can understand. I'm bewildered."

Irma's voice was husky, too! She seemed to have all the

equipment of a cocotte. Very different from her mother, who was a real good sort. Perhaps Irma's seductive side came from her father, the cabby!

"Have you any idea why your husband should commit suicide?"

"I haven't. He must have gone mad."

"Was he hard-up? You remember, he was wrong in his cash at the bank."

"I can't tell what to think. He never said he was short of money. In fact, we'd money put-by. I have it here upstairs. National Savings and a Post Office account. And, after all, to a decent bank cashier, his cash is sacred. Cyril was like the rest. Honest and meticulous. As I said, he must have gone temporarily off his head."

"Why?"

"I don't know. We were happy together. . . ."

Her mother gave her a quick, challenging look for just a second. It was an instinctive gesture and she gave Little-john a sly glance after it to make sure he hadn't seen it. He was filling his pipe.

Irma couldn't stop acting. Gesticulating and striking poses. Sometimes, it reminded you of the silent films where the actors made exaggerated movements because they couldn't speak. Only Irma talked twenty to the dozen.

"He always gave me enough to save something. He was a bit extravagant himself, so passed on to me what he could spare to take care of. . . ."

If what Irma said was true, she'd inherited a thrifty streak from her mother.

"Did he make you a dress allowance?"

She flared-up magnificently. Anger . . . and yet a little pride that he'd noticed her clothes.

"Are you suggesting that I dress above what we could afford?"

"No. But. . . ."

Mrs. Utting was getting anxious. This was no way to speak to a policeman. Especially one so nice mannered and understanding as the Superintendent.

"Don't you start getting indignant, Irma. The Super. is only trying to help us, I'm sure. He won't ask you silly questions. Just answer him civil. . . ."

"Well, I won't have it said I made Cyril hard-up and worried by spending too much on clothes. I have friends in the fashion-trade and they give me dresses and shoes and even underwear sometimes. When they're admired, it's part of the bargain that I say where they came from, the brands etcetera."

"You never said anything about it to me."

"I don't go all over the place, mother, telling people my clothes are given or borrowed."

"Did your husband give you a weekly or monthly dress allowance, too?"

"Yes. And he'd some to spare after it. I didn't fling my money about. I saved a bit, as I said before. If Cyril was hard-up, or even short in his cash, he'd come to me and I'd see him through. It's my opinion that cash shortage was just a careless mistake he made."

A thousand pounds! Just a mistake!

"But he had a reputation for care and accuracy, hadn't he?"

"We can't be perfect all the time, can we?"

"You said he came to you when he was wrong in his cash. Has he been wrong before, then?"

"Odd pounds, now and then. . . ."

"But don't the bank make such differences right?"

"Cyril once told me they did. But he never liked to report shortages. Perhaps he was too proud, or maybe afraid he'd be moved off the counter. He dreaded the idea of ever not being a cashier."

"Did you ever suspect he might be blackmailed, Mrs. Bastable?"

She looked back at him open-mouthed.

"Blackmail! Cyril! Whatever for? He'd no secrets anybody could turn into cash. The idea's ridiculous. He was the last person to get involved."

"He didn't have any women friends?"

Irma laughed outright and her mother smiled slowly.

"Are you suggesting that Cyril might have been unfaithful to me? And robbed the bank to keep up his second establishment? It's too ridiculous! He wasn't that sort at all. We were always happy and he was satisfied with me, I know."

But Irma hadn't been satisfied with Cyril, from all accounts. You'd only to see her to know that. A sensual, sophisticated adventuress like Irma. . . . It was obvious.

Mrs. Utting rose and made for the door.

"I'll leave you two together while I make a cup of tea."

"Please don't trouble, Mrs. Utting."

"No trouble at all. I couldn't think of letting you go without a drink. Perhaps you'd like some whisky. I've got a bottle in the dining-room."

"Tea will be fine, thank you."

Irma was sitting opposite him now. Knees together, back straight. She'd been taught to behave like a lady by her mother. The scent came across in gentle waves.

"Did you know a man called Plaster?"

Her eyes grew large.

"The disgusting little man who was drowned in the canal?"

"Yes."

"He used to hang about at our dramatic society at Barnet. He did the painting and scene-shifting. And he owned a building we used as a boat-club on the canal at Berkhampstead. We do a lot of boating there in the summer-time. As I said, he owned the building and used to take advantage of it to come down when we were all there, get drunk on the whisky some of the men brought and paid for, and then throw his weight about and get offensive. Cyril told him off a time or two."

"You heard him?"

"Not exactly. But Plaster once or twice made a pass at me. A horrible man. I told Cyril and he said he'd speak to him. When I asked him, he said he'd done it."

"You know the Falconers and the Myerses very well?"

"Yes. They didn't live far from us at Barnet. They were neighbours and in the same bank and we saw quite a lot of them. In fact, we introduced them in the dramatic society and the canal-club."

"You lived in your own house at Barnet?"

"No. A flat. It's a largish house made into two flats. The landlord lived in the lower one."

"You run a car?"

"A small one."

"There are garages at the flats?"

"Yes. At the side. It holds two cars; one for each tenant."

"What is the address?"

"I'd have thought you'd know it. Selborne, Abbey Crescent, Barnet. Do you wish to see over it?"

It was said quite innocently. But then, a lot of Irma's tactics sounded quite innocent.

"Not just now, thanks. But I'll note the address."

He wrote it on an old envelope. He could hardly keep a straight face. Irma must be used to this kind of thing. Telephone numbers and one rendezvous after another written in diaries and on bits of paper. All the same, he had to confess that it might have given many a man quite a thrill.

"Where were you and your husband on the evening of May 25th, Mrs. Bastable?"

"Why that date?"

"It was the date on which Plaster met his death."

"But surely, you don't think . . . ?"

"No. I wondered if either or both of you were down at *The Bargees' Rest* that evening. Plaster might have been there. I'd like to know what condition he was in."

"I'm sure I can't say whether or not we were there. It's so long ago. Most likely Cyril was. He often went in the evening tinkering with his boat. We have a little boat . . . just a teeny one. . . ."

She gave the impression of teeniness by measuring an inch between her outstretched thumb and forefinger, as though the boat might have been a piece of cake!

". . . with an outboard motor."

"You didn't always go with him?"

"Of course not. I've other things to do. I can't spend every evening messing about the canal. Besides, all Cyril's painting and playing with the machinery just bored me. Sometimes, on week-nights, there'd be nobody else there. I like company. Hanging around the empty club and boat-house would just have driven me round the bend."

Mrs. Utting entered with a round silver-plated tea-tray of the kind they used to give away for hundreds of tea coupons, and a teapot and other accessories to match. A plateful of biscuits, too, with coloured icing on them. She poured out the tea with dignity and passed it round and then she took a drink herself, her little finger held upright as she did so.

She looked hard at her daughter. There were questions in the glance. "Have you behaved like a lady? Is everything all right?"

They sat there, eating and drinking, all cosy and nice.

"Poor Cyril," said Mrs. Utting at length, in a kindly cheer-ful voice, as though she might have been encouraging her late son-in-law somewhere in the shades.

"To think that he should come to such an end."

Irma sighed as well and ate another biscuit.

"Life goes on. . . ."

Her voice failed very slightly as she said it.

Littlejohn glanced round the commonplace little lounge. It had probably all started there. Cyril and Irma canoodling in the dark, a quick marriage, and disillusionment as quick for poor Cyril. He'd lost heart and gradually deteriorated, finally ending-up on the slab in the morgue . . . a suicide. And now here was Irma, getting ready for her next adventure.

Mrs. Utting looked at him mournfully. If Irma hadn't been there, she might easily have ended up in having a good cry in Littlejohn's company. She couldn't quite under-stand it all. She'd had her fun in a taxi-cab years ago, and paid for it. Then, she'd gone straight and concentrated on trying to bring up Irma properly. She'd tried to make a lady of her and even now, she gave her a look of quiet pride.

But she couldn't understand why the girl didn't show more grief. Why, even after Utting died in hospital after falling in the fire, she'd cried every time she'd thought of him for over twelve months. Irma, on the contrary, was blooming and thriving on her widowhood. . . .

" Is there anything more, sir? "

She was beginning to feel a bit ashamed of Irma's attitude. She might have shed a tear or two in front of the Superintendent if only for the look of things. . . . And now, she seemed to be waiting for something. . . .

Outside a large car was drawing-up at the front door. It was enormous. Almost as big as a pantechnicon. A man jumped out, knocked on the door, and then stood on the door-step admiring the monstrous vehicle. He wore flannels, a pullover, had a small moustache and a spreading, loose mouth.

Mrs. Utting looked embarrassed, but Irma took it all in her stride.

" It's Leslie. . . . He promised to take me up to London. I've some shopping to do."

Littlejohn shook hands with Irma and she gave his hand a warm significant squeeze. Her mother had gone to let Leslie in. They could hear her taking him in the dining-room behind as though ashamed to bring him in to Littlejohn.

Irma spoke to Littlejohn in an earnest whisper, sharing with the Superintendent a secret unknown to her mother.

" Please excuse mother, if she seems dazed. She was very fond of Cyril. . . ."

" Weren't you? "

" Of course. But then our generation isn't so demonstrative and sentimental, is it? "

And Littlejohn almost old enough to be her father!

" Was Leslie, who's just arrived, a friend of Mr. Bastable? "

" No. Leslie lives in Brighton. I don't think Cyril knew him. He's an auctioneer and estate agent. Leslie Peppercorn and Wallis. Perhaps you've heard of them? "

C

" I can't say I have."

" He's been very kind to me in my bereavement. . . ."

In the other room, Peppercorn's voice was booming at Mrs. Utting as though he were selling her a lot of cattle or old furniture at an auction-sale.

Littlejohn thoughtfully filled his pipe on the way up Chisholm Street to the station. A large policeman was coming in the opposite direction looking annoyed.

" I've told Peppercorn before about parking his cinema organ in Chisholm Street. Now I'll book him. . . ."

Littlejohn stopped him and introduced himself.

" How long has this been going on? "

" Peppercorn and Mrs. Bastable, you mean? Since Christmas. Long before her husband committed suicide. No wonder he shot himself. . . ."

The whole thing might easily have been a farce, if Littlejohn hadn't suddenly become securely aware, with the unfailing instinct of an old hand, that he had run right into the unholy atmosphere of murder.

6

SATURDAY AFTERNOON

THE BARGEES' REST had, when it was a halting-place for water traffic, been called *The Old Cock*. For some facetious reason, the Barnet gang had re-named it when they took it over. It stood squeezed in a cutting facing the canal, with only the tow-path between. It wasn't a large place. Low-lying, two up and two down, with a kind of courtyard behind it where the brewery lorries had once unloaded beer into the cellars, and where, in early days, cock-fighting had gone on in its natural amphitheatre.

It was Saturday afternoon and Littlejohn had been kept late at the Yard on a case. He'd had to ring-up Falconer, who had arranged to take him to the canal in his car, and tell him he'd make his own way there by taxi.

"It's not hard to find, sir. And I'll take you home after-wards," Falconer had said in his now familiar drawling voice.

It was three o'clock when Littlejohn arrived. They went through Berkhampstead and then turned off into the narrow, sunken, unmetalled road, once used by the drays for reaching the inn with the beer. They were soon there.

The weather held. Hot and sunny, with hardly a breath of air. It was cooler, however, by the canal.

Everything was in full-blast. About a score of people there, some of them paddling around in canoes, others resting in deck-chairs on the bank. A number of them had gone off in their motor-boats and on the opposite side, a young man, clad in nothing but a pair of swimming briefs, was struggling with the engine of his boat. Myers was there with his wife and two young boys—the water-babies—one of whom had an air-gun and was trying to shoot sparrows; the other was eating an ice-cream.

Falconer was dressed in a white shirt, shorts, and wore a canvas cap with a large peak. He was sprawling serenely in a wicker chair, smoking cigarettes and watching the assorted craft passing on the water. When he saw Littlejohn he waved, rose languidly, and came to meet him in his slow, gangling, long-legged way, and shook hands.

"Glad you made it. Come and meet some friends. You'll know quite a few of them. There aren't as many here as usual. Half the members are on holiday."

"This is Fleur, my wife. . . ."

She was sitting in a chair next to Falconer's, with a long drink on the table at her side. Littlejohn couldn't help comparing her with Irma, whom he'd met the day before. Fleur was as cool, temperamentally, as Irma was hot. In her white frock, brown-haired, pink complexioned, fine featured, she was more beautiful than Irma, but there was none of the other woman's sparkle and vitality. Fleur was almost as languid as her husband, greeted Littlejohn with a calm handshake and a faint smile, and then sat down again.

"Hadn't you better get the Superintendent a drink, darling, and bring some water for Cain and Abel at the same time?"

Littlejohn then noticed two white poodles tied to the table-leg, lying under it in the shade, exhausted and panting in the heat.

She said it politely and then fished in a white miniature kit-bag beside her on the gravel and brought out a piece of embroidery, after struggling to extricate it from the rest of the contents. Fleur smoothed it out on the table and then the same struggle occurred as she sorted out the coloured silks from a confused tangle, which she drew from the bag and which looked like a mass of many-dyed spaghetti.

Falconer was back, carrying bottles of beer with cold beads of condensation on them, and glasses. He was holding, too, a bowl full of water. He bent and put it before the poodles, who began to lap it eagerly, growling at one another.

"The beer's cool. We've got a refrigerator inside the *Rest*."

" I can't unravel these silks, dear. Get me out the magenta,
the lime-green, and the sky-blue."

Falconer didn't know what to do first. Eventually, he
sorted out the colours quickly and carefully with his useful
hands, and then he opened the beer, poured it, and passed
a glass to Littlejohn. Fleur eyed the drinks greedily.

" I could drink a nice beer myself. This Martini's quite
warm."

Falconer went and brought one, unperturbed, good tem-
pered, slowly as ever. But Littlejohn saw he was seeking an
excuse for release.

" Let's go and meet the others, shall we? "

Under the table the dogs began to yap at each other
and Falconer had to bend and quieten them before
he left.

He led the way, after lighting a cigarette and one for his
wife, who called him back to give it to her.

First, the Myerses. Myers himself in a thin shirt, shorts,
barelegged, sandals on his feet. A different Myers from the
one at the bank. Here he was secretary of the club, the com-
mandant of the Moorgate Navy. He took his duties gravely.
His hands were covered in oil from repairing the engine of
young Vance, who owned a little second-hand boat in which
he'd now chugged-off in triumph for a run with Miss
Browning.

" Care to come inside, Superintendent, while I clean up,
and I'll show you over the place? "

Falconer made an excuse to leave them. Fleur was calling.
The dogs were scrapping again.

" Pity about poor Falconer. His wife can't bear him out
of her sight for long. Can't do a thing for herself. And as
for those damned poodles. . . . They'll kill one another one
day. . . . Come and meet the wife and boys. Remember, I told
you we called them the water-babies. The eldest, a girl,
has gone to a guide rally today. They've all been brought up
here. Love the place."

A homely little woman, once pretty, now a bit fagged with
looking after the children, Myers, and other things. She was

president of this and that in the way of good works; Institutes, dramatic societies, girl guides, animal welfare. . . . She was now talking about getting tea ready for the whole party.

The Myers kids were a couple of little horrors. The elder had pulled the younger's clockwork motor-boat to pieces and scattered the bits far and wide. The younger was howling his head off.

" Say good afternoon to the gentleman."

No answer.

Myers stood at the door of *The Bargees' Rest* and indicated the scene to Littlejohn with a wave of the hand.

" Pretty, isn't it? "

Country houses and villas behind the far bank. Somewhere somebody was playing tennis and they could hear the calls and the dull thud of the balls. Almost opposite, the grounds of a mansion came right down to the water's edge and facing the canal was a summer-house in which an old man was asleep in a deck-chair.

" We did all this ourselves. . . ."

A white painted exterior with a pale-blue door. They'd even had electricity installed and a telephone.

" Not a bad place, eh? "

Myers was proud of it. He wasn't much in the dramatic society, but when it came to something practical or to do with sailing, he was in his element.

It was the same indoors. All neat with white paint and clean and tidy. A kind of common-room with wicker chairs and little tables for when it rained or for after dark, and then two separate dressing-rooms for men and women. Behind, a small kitchen.

" We've installed a cooker and a refrigerator. . . ."

They entered the men's room and Myers washed his strong hairy arms in hot water at one of the washbowls. On one wall a number of lockers each with its owner's name. Littlejohn quickly spotted that of Bastable. *C. Bastable,* on a card in a little brass frame. It was locked.

" Has this been opened since he died? "

"No. In the confusion it was forgotten and we didn't like to upset Irma by mentioning it so soon after. She probably has the key, although I have duplicates in my locker. Do you want to look inside?"

"If you please?"

Myers opened his own locker, pulled out a bunch of keys, all of which looked alike, selected one, and opened Bastable's.

There was little in it. A spanner, a hammer, some screw-keys and odds and ends of wire, sparking-plugs and accessories for tinkering with motors. An old white jacket, and a half-empty bottle of whisky right in the centre of the cupboard.

"Poor old Bastable. The last time he'll drink here. We buy our own drinks—no licence—but we share them out on a kind of co-operative basis, you know. . . ."

"Did Bastable drink a lot?"

"Now and then, he'd take rather a lot when he got a fit of the blues. Otherwise, he wasn't a heavy drinker."

"Did he often get the blues?"

"He was rather a melancholy sort of chap. He just couldn't keep up with Irma. She's so full of vitality. The life and soul of the party. He always struck me as very short of energy and go. . . ."

He stretched out his hand to the whisky bottle.

"Please don't, sir."

Littlejohn picked it up by the cork and examined it.

"This may be useful to us. I don't know. But I'd like to take it."

Myers looked a bit rattled. All this fuss because some teddy-boy or other had talked about Bastable on his death-bed! He thought the police were kicking-up a lot of undue fuss.

"Perhaps you'll lock the bottle in again and I'll ask you for it before I leave."

"All right. I'll tell Irma you want it, when she comes. She's expected this afternoon. She likes it down here and it'll take her mind off her troubles. She's good company.

Before this tragedy, she often brought a record-player with her and we'd dance in the evenings when the boats were all in."

Myers's eyes sparkled at the thought of it. He, too, had evidently pleasant memories of Irma in spite of his family preoccupations.

They went outside again. As they passed the common-room, they could see Mrs. Myers and one or two others laying the little tables for tea.

The canal was alive with activity. Sailing, rowing, fishing. Motor-boats slowly gliding past. In the distance someone was playing a gramophone. *We'll gather lilacs in the spring again.* . . . All very pleasant and sentimental. Littlejohn thought about Bastable, wrong in his cash, fretted by his wife's incessant flirtations, hag-ridden by his melancholy streak. . . . The sight of all this happiness was enough to drive him mad.

Myers took Littlejohn in tow, introducing him here and there to members of his own little gang, mainly bank people. There were others there, but they moved genially in their own sets. The Superintendent was described as a friend of Falconer's who'd been invited to see the place. Nothing was said about Bastable, although at first, many of the party regarded Littlejohn with curiosity. They all soon became familiar, however. Everybody behaved with the exaggerated friendliness which prevails in such clubs. Another visit or two, and they'd be calling Littlejohn by his Christian name, too.

Falconer waved to Littlejohn. He was in mid-stream, rowing Myers's youngest round in a small canoe. Practically every family seemed to have a boat of some sort. When they all came home to roost at night, there would be a crowd too big for the *Rest* to accommodate.

Carr, the assistant-manager of the bank, was back. He was steering-in a sumptuous little cabin-cruiser owned by a man with a mansion higher up the canal and reputed to be a millionaire. His daughter was with Carr, a tall, angular, eager, fair girl, with her hair swept back into a pony-tail.

They tied-up the boat and disembarked and the girl imme-
diately left him to greet her friends. She was giggling. She
and Carr had evidently been mixing drinks on their
journey. Carr himself was much more genial with Littlejohn
than when they'd first met at the bank.

"Talk to the Superintendent for a minute or two, Roger,"
said Myers, "while I open some tins of tongue for my wife.
She's busy with the tea."

Carr offered Littlejohn a drink.

"There's plenty on the boat. Sally's father does himself
well. The thing's a floating pub. . . ."

He glared over the water at Falconer who was now across
stream, impeding the traffic.

"I wish Falconer wouldn't be so damned casual on the
water. It's bad enough when he's on terra firma. . . . Look
at him now. Rowing the boat round and round just to please
the kid. Well . . . I guess one mustn't complain. It's the only
time he really enjoys himself when he's playing with somebody's kids. The rest of the time, he's waiting on Fleur or
else tippling. He retires in four years. What he'll do, God
knows. Retirement with Fleur will kill him. Dreary desola-
tion. She's as pretty as a picture and that's all you can say
for her. . . ."

Carr was half-drunk and it was becoming embarrassing.
Suddenly relief. . . .

Irma had arrived. The huge car swung its way down the
old road and appeared like a great animal behind *The
Bargees' Rest*. Peppercorn was at the wheel. The pair of
them were wearing sunglasses and looked ready for the
Riviera.

"Who the devil's Irma got this time?"

Carr sounded annoyed.

"Excuse me. Must offer condolences. Not seen Irma since
Bastable died. . . ."

Myers was back and Carr hurried to the pantechnicon to
greet her.

"Now for the fun. The women'll be furious. She always
gets here in time for tea but never lends a hand."

c*

Peppercorn was being introduced and Irma was making excuses for bringing him.

"He's attending to the sale of the house in Barnet. I can't stay there now. We were down looking it over and I thought we might get a spot of tea here before we go back to Brighton. . . ."

The gathering had started to bubble over with good humour. Irma seemed to have livened everything up. She was in a smart white turnout relieved by a black scarf. Peppercorn had brought some champagne.

"Got to pay my whack, you know."

He wore a thin shirt, flannels, and a coloured neckcloth tucked under the collar of his shirt. A large, swarthy, flabby fellow of forty or so, with all the effrontery and self-confidence in the world.

Falconer landed and lifted out the child, who began to whimper for another spell on the water. He turned him over to someone else and slouched off to join his wife. Since Littlejohn arrived Falconer had drunk enough to put an ordinary man on his back, but he was perfectly steady. He ignored the arrival of Irma and they could hear his wife asking him politely to get her some of Peppercorn's champagne which was being opened.

A thin, half-naked little man with large ears and black-framed spectacles, and a plump woman in a white costume drew alongside in a natty little motor-boat and jumped ashore. Nobody greeted them. On the contrary, they were cold-shouldered.

"What's going on? Champagne? Better get me a glass, Henry."

Conversation on all sides. People wandering from group to group. Irma was flashing her eyes at Carr, who was talking earnestly with her. Falconer was struggling with the dogs again, keeping them apart whilst he fed them with biscuits.

Littlejohn, sitting calmly waiting for Falconer to return, looked round at the happy family. Somewhere among them was the explanation of Bastable's desperate act in killing

Plaster and the suicide which followed it. His eyes fell on Irma, Peppercorn, Carr and Myers in turn. And then on Falconer, busy keeping the dogs quiet.

Irma and Carr were still talking. Now they seemed to be quarrelling. Peppercorn wandering around with a tray of little tumblers filled with champagne. He'd settled down as one of the party. The wine was beginning to take effect. People chattering, laughing, drinking. . . . Some of them were hardly aware of what they were saying or doing. Irma was still tête à tête with Carr. They were friends again now. He was so enthralled that he could hardly keep his hands off her.

" It's scandalous. . . ."

It came from the plump woman who had landed with the little man with the ears. They were sitting apart from the rest and had evidently been drinking before they arrived.

Littlejohn sipped his champagne, idly watching the passing craft; a skiff rowed by two long young men, a canoe paddled by an earnest-looking girl with buck teeth and spectacles, and a little boat with an outboard motor chugging slowly along.

" It's scandalous. . . ."

She repeated it and when Littlejohn turned in her direction, she turned as well and addressed him like an old friend.

" She's finished with Carr now for somebody else with more money—the chap dishing out the champagne by the bucketful."

" Dry-up, Ethel. Somebody'll hear you."

" Dry-up yourself. And I don't care who hears me. It's true, isn't it? They say poor Bastable shot himself because he'd robbed the bank. More likely because he couldn't make his wife behave herself. When he died, it was Carr. Now it's Pitchpine. . . ."

" Peppercorn, Ethel, and keep your voice down."

" Pitchpine or Peppercorn, it's all the same to me. And shut-up when I'm talking to the gentleman. Pity Bastable wasn't alive now. He'd be able to touch Pitchpine for a loan, too."

Littlejohn lit his pipe.

" A loan? "

" Of course. I've been a member here from the start. My late husband owned *The Bargees' Rest*, as they call it. Now, it's mine. I'm an honorary member. . . ."

So, this was Mrs. Plaster! No wonder the gang snubbed her.

" She's had four of them, one after another. And poor Mr. Bastable touched them all. I saw it done. At the dramatic society while my husband was scene painting. They didn't see me, but I heard Bastable say to Bradburn that he was at his wits' end for money. His wife spent all he'd got and he couldn't bear not keeping her in the way she'd been kept before he married her. The way she'd been kept! You can see that without asking. Bastable was whining and wheedling and smiling that beaten smile of his. Did you know Bradburn? "

" No. . . ."

" He was a stockbroker who did a bit of acting. He left the club after Irma gave him the cold shoulder, though they were as thick as thieves till somebody better turned-up. Bastable used to get loans out of them. Permanent ones without interest, if you get what I mean. Blackmail. That's what it was."

She turned to the man with the ears.

" Get me another glass of champagne before it's all gone."

" Haven't you had enough, Ethel? "

" Right. If you won't, I will."

She rose and unsteadily sought out Peppercorn. The man she'd left behind gave Littlejohn a sidelong glance.

" Don't take any notice of Ethel. She can't take a drink. Two . . . and she's sunk. Talks a lot of rubbish."

" Is she Mrs. Plaster? "

" Yes. As she said, since her husband died, she's inherited *The Bargees' Rest*. I told her not to land here. We're not wanted, you know. Not their class. But she insisted. She more

or less gets her own way because she's the landlord and
they're the tenants and they've got no lease."

Ethel was back.

"They tell me you're a detective. What happened? Why
are you down here?"

"I came on the invitation of Mr. Falconer. Purely
social."

"Don't give me that. I wasn't born yesterday. I could tell
you a thing or two about this lot. And I've got a nice little
puzzle for you to solve. . . . It's in a book my husband
left."

She nodded owlishly.

"Yes, I'm going home now. Can't stand this lot. Snobs,
that's what they are. And they'll have to mind their p's and
q's the way they treat me, or else they'll be out. If you'll
come along, I'll show you the book I told you about. Henry,
here, and me've had too much to drink to drive ourselves.
You're the police and you don't catch me that way and book
me. You can drive us. I'll show you the book then."

"All right."

Littlejohn apologized to Falconer and said good-bye to the
rest. He wanted an excuse to go. He was like a fish out of
water and doing no good hanging about.

"I've work still to do."

Falconer accepted it in his usual easygoing way.

"Come again, then. Any time. Just let me know and I'll
pick you up and bring you."

"Thanks. Mrs. Plaster's offered me a lift."

"Don't admire your choice. Let me run you back."

"No, thanks. It would be a pity to disturb you when she's
going my way."

"Has she introduced you to Henry? He's her boy-friend.
Has been since long before Plaster fell in the canal. She runs
the shop and Henry runs another, a health-food store right
opposite. Well, *au revoir*, then."

"*Au revoir*, Mr. Falconer. Thanks for the afternoon out."

Mrs. Plaster signalled that she was ready and led the way
to a smart little car, parked behind *The Bargees' Rest*.

" Here's the key."

Littlejohn started the engine and they drove off. Ethel sat beside Littlejohn showing him the way to South Mimms.

Henry took the back seat and at once fell asleep.

7

PLASTER'S LITTLE BOOK

ETHEL PLASTER DIDN'T stop talking all the way. When she wasn't telling Littlejohn the way to South Mimms by a series of short cuts, she was busy running-down the members of *The Bargees' Club*.

"A lot of snobs, they are, with little money and a lot of swank. Plaster could have bought the lot of them up, and now that his money's come to me, I could do the same. . . . Turn right here and then go left at the first opening. . . ."

Henry slept through it all; now and then he'd break into snores, wake himself, turn over, and go off again.

"My late husband and me were connected with the stage before we set-up in business. I was a dancer and he was a property-man. He was always interested in furniture. He knew good stuff when he saw it and after we'd started in the trade, he used to go to sales and buy. He'd quite a good connection with antique dealers in the West-End. Bear right all the way from here. . . ."

"And that's how you came to meet the dramatic society. You lent them properties?"

"Yes. They came to borrow furniture for some show or other. Plaster took it along and gave them the benefit of his stage experience. I went with him sometimes. Once the stage is in your blood, you know, it seems to draw you."

"And Henry. . . . Who's he? A relative?"

"Mr. Dancer, you mean. He has a health-food shop that he runs with his sister not far from ours. He's a bachelor and a bit lonely, and me and Plaster got friendly with him."

Littlejohn could imagine it all. There had probably, as Falconer suggested, been an affair going on between Dancer

and Mrs. Plaster before her husband died. She had a posses-
sive way with Henry which couldn't be mistaken.

Under the declining influence of the champagne, Mrs.
Plaster was still confidentially disposed

"Henry suggested him and me might get married after a
respectful time from Plaster's death. But I said, no. Friends,
yes. But after the way me and my late husband worked and
made our money and independence, I'm not allowing any
other man to hang up his hat with me and take possession of
the business. . . . Turn left at the end, and we're there. I'll
show you the shop."

F. Plaster
Modern and Antique Furniture
Bought and Sold

It was a large shop with two windows filled with furniture
of all kinds. Odds and ends of china here and there, a glass
case containing coins, and some old pistols displayed in the
window-bottoms.

Henry was awake. He made to follow Mrs. Plaster and
Littlejohn, but Ethel stopped him.

"You'd better go home, Henry. I'll see you later on. Call
round about eight."

Dancer didn't seem to mind. Ethel was obviously in full
control of their arrangements. He bade Littlejohn a civil
good-bye and rather unsteadily wobbled across the road to
the health-food shop which was visible from the Plasters'
doorstep.

Dancer's Health Stores
Herbal Remedies Sold

Mrs. Plaster took a key from her handbag and opened the
door. There was a cardboard sign behind the glass panel.
CLOSED. She reversed it to show she was in. OPEN.

"Come in. This way. . . ."

She led the way through a confusion of furniture of all

kinds. Chairs piled up, wardrobes with their backs to the walls practically all round the shop, china cabinets, bookcases, escritoires, armchairs, dressing-tables. . . . All well-kept and not much of it could be described as junk.

They entered a small room at the back. The livingquarters. Quite a cosy place and filled with good furniture sufficient for the needs of a man and wife.

"This room is always changing. We keep the best stuff here and use it for a bit. Then it goes out, mostly to antique dealers."

She took off her shoes first, and then rubbed her feet.

"My poor feet. This warm weather tries them up a bit. You'll excuse me?"

She put on a pair of old slippers. Then she removed her costume coat. She looked better then. She had plump white arms and an ample figure.

"Shall I make some tea?"

"If you're having some yourself, I wouldn't mind a cup, Mrs. Plaster. . . ."

She busied herself in a scullery at the back and soon was back with a tray with beautiful Worcester china on it and a cake.

Another good sort. Not very far removed from Mrs. Utting, but being comfortably off in the way of cash had made her more independent and self-confident. She poured out the tea and passed the cake.

"I don't want to waste your time, Superintendent, but when I saw you down at the canal and heard who you were, I just wondered if the police are thinking the same as me."

"And what is that?"

"That maybe Plaster's death wasn't an accident at all."

"What makes you think that, Mrs. Plaster?"

"Just that I can't believe that Fred, my husband, although he took more drink than was good for him, would have been so silly as to walk in the canal and get drowned. The things I've seen that man do while under the influence were surprising. If he could walk straight across a road alive with traffic . . . Yes, and he once climbed on the roof here . . . dead drunk, mind you . . . to bring down a cat that had run there out of the way of some dogs and couldn't get down. . . . He wasn't likely to walk in the canal."

"What do you think happened, then?"

"I think somebody pushed him in. He couldn't swim. Or else, made him unconscious and threw him in."

"With what motive?"

She took a good drink of her tea and then filled-up both their cups.

"I'll be quite candid about it. If it got about that my late husband had been murdered, Henry Dancer might be on a spot. It's known that he's been sweet on me for a long time. He even suggested I should leave Fred and go away with him. But this life suits me. And Henry wouldn't harm a fly. So that leaves others."

"Others. Who might they be?"

"That's why I invited you here. If you've finished your tea, I'll show you. Come this way."

She took him back in the shop, in the gloom of which was a small office. An old dingy place where you needed a light on to see your way about. Just an old desk, a chair, and a safe in one corner.

Mrs. Plaster took out her keys again.

"My late husband always carried the keys of the safe himself. I never knew what was in it. And when his keys came to me after he died and I opened it up, there wasn't much exciting there. Some money, his account books, and this. . . .

She'd opened the door and had now in her hand a cheap little greasy dog-eared note-book. She passed it over to Littlejohn.

"You might as well take a look at it. There's not much private in it."

Littlejohn sat on the chair by the desk and turned the pages.

The book was about a quarter full of figures and what

must have been Plaster's sprawling and illiterate hand-writing. Each page had a name at the top, but they were all nicknames, a kind of code.

"What would you say all this was, Mrs. Plaster?"

"The names, you mean? I think they're transactions he wanted to keep secret. So, in case anybody got his book at any time, he gave nicknames to the people he was dealing with. He'd a queer sense of humour. Whenever he met any-body, he'd fix on their peculiarity and call them after it. For instance, although I shouldn't make fun of a friend, he used to call Henry, Mr. Dancer, 'Mutton Chops' because he was a vegetarian, and Mr. Hamlet, next door, 'Father's Ghost'. . . . You see what I mean? It was, in a sort of way, like cockney slang, wasn't it?"

Littlejohn was examining the entries in the book. Each name had a column of figures beneath it, beginning with a round sum, which frequently declined by fixed instalments. Sometimes, it increased by an added amount. And, as far as Littlejohn could see, the initial item had interest added at the start. The interest rate, on a rough calculation, was in the region of twenty-five per cent.

"He was a moneylender, Mrs. Plaster?"

"To tell you the truth, Superintendent, he was. He thought I didn't know. But I did. People used to call here and talk to him in this very office. At first, I wondered if it was something shady in the trade, but the types who used to come weren't that sort. They were the hard-up, borrowing kind. You know what I mean."

"Yes. But surely your husband had some kind of security. He didn't just write a nickname and the amount in a book and leave it at that."

"No, he didn't. He took notes of hand. Sort of promissory notes. And he always carried those notes about in his pocket-book. It was bulging with them. He wasn't going to have anybody burgling the shop and taking his securities. I know, because once, when he drank himself into the D.T.'s, they brought him home and I had to undress him. I took the chance to have a look in his pocket-book, which I'd noticed made a big bulge in his jacket. I thought it was cash. Instead, I found the notes. That's some years ago. I can't remember the names. Nobody I knew."

"When his clothes were returned after the inquest, was the pocket-book there with the notes in it?"

"No. That's another reason why I think there's something fishy about his death. He might have been murdered by somebody who couldn't pay-up and was likely to get in trouble for it. Mr. Plaster, you know, was a hard man where business was concerned."

"But why was he so secretive about his moneylending?"

"He wasn't a registered moneylender, of course. I think he started it on the side to help his friends. . . ."

Friends! At twenty-five per cent interest! That was a good one!

". . . Have you seen the interest he charged, too? I don't know much about loans, but I'm sure that's not legal. If it went to court, he'd have to pay some of it back. He might even have gone to gaol for usury. Don't you think so?"

"He'd have got in hot water."

"So, it was secret between him and borrowers. Perhaps they were people who couldn't raise money elsewhere, because they were so hard-up. They would be the sort who'd do him in if he threatened them with some hold he'd got over them."

"Such as telling their employers and getting them into trouble?"

"You've got me. That's it."

She spoke of the dead man with no respect at all. In fact, you'd guess that she despised him.

"He got drinking far too much. I ran the shop; he did the buying. And in the end, I'd go to sales myself to keep the business together. He just drank and drank and, from the looks of things, lent money at high rates. Towards the finish, he never gave me any money. Anything I wanted, I made in the shop. I don't like mean people."

She seemed a decent sort and she'd obviously been good-looking in her own way when she was younger. In spite of her abundant bosom, fat arms and legs, and bad feet, there were still traces of the dark, lively girl she'd been in her dancing days. She was good-hearted, too. That was obvious from the way she took sides with her husband's borrowers against Plaster himself.

"I suppose these poor devils will be relieved to know that Plaster won't screw them any more. The notes have gone, there's only the book, and I don't propose to solve the riddles of the names and start dunning them. I only thought the book might give you a clue."

"Let's take down the names, then."

Littlejohn picked up a pencil from the desk and an invoice with Plaster's name and occupation on the top, and began to write.

There were only eight names, presumably those of outstanding borrowers. Quite a number had been crossed out, probably after paying-off their debts. The rest. . . .

Humpy	£ 50	Bimbo	£765
One Lung	34	Cuckoo	56
Carrot	130	Red	300
Crusoe	15	Spider	125

"Do these suggest anything to you, Mrs. Plaster?"

She smiled.

"Well, I must say I've been very interested in those names since I found the book. I think I've guessed some of them. But what beats me is why Plaster should conceal their identities the way he did. I admit, he'd got queer and secretive. In fact, it was the drink did it."

"His health didn't seem to have suffered much, though. The post mortem didn't reveal heart trouble or even liver degeneration."

"He hadn't been drinking heavy before this year. Then he seemed to go all to pieces and was never hardly sober."

"You were going to tell me what you found out about the nicknames."

"Yes. I'm sure Humpy was a hunchbacked man who used to slip in secretly and talk for hours in this very office. Plaster might have lent him money. And I'm certain One Lung is the carter who used to do some furniture moving for us. He'd been in a sanatorium at one time and once told me he'd only one lung. . . ."

"Small sums, those, weren't they?"

"Yes. But you'd see from the ins and outs on their accounts, they were always in Plaster's debt. They've owed him money for years."

"That's right. Regular customers."

"Carrot, I wouldn't know. I didn't know all my husband's friends. He met some of them in pubs, you see. Crusoe's somebody called Robinson, I'd think."

"A good guess. But look at Bimbo. He's the best customer, but his account shows very little repayment. It's piled-up over the past three years with nothing in the way of payments off. Bimbo. . . . That's a queer name. And yet, it sounds familiar."

"He was a famous clown, wasn't he?"

"That's right, Mrs. Plaster! You've hit it! I saw him in a circus when I was a boy. This borrower must have struck your husband as looking like a clown or behaving like one, so he gave the name to him. Who could that be? Know anyone like a clown?"

"Plenty. But not the sort Plaster would lend seven hundred pounds to."

"Did he never mention anybody being or looking like a clown?"

"Not to my recollection. I'll try to think. Red, I fancy I know, too. He was a communist who set-up in business as a greengrocer in South Mimms. I remember him coming here to see Plaster. I never liked him. He's the one I'd make pay-up if I was that way inclined. But he's got a hard-working wife and four kids, so I'll let it go. Spider. . . . I've never heard of him. Unpleasant sort of name."

" Perhaps he's called Webb."

" Maybe. I don't know the name. If your police cared to call at some of the pubs Plaster used, they might get a line on one or two. Cuckoo, too, is a queer name. Cuckoo in the nest, someone gone cuckoo, or maybe. . . ."

She smiled again.

" Maybe he's a cuckoo on account of his wife."

Like Plaster, judging from Henry's obvious position in the family! Littlejohn instinctively thought of Bastable, too.

" Let me see the book again. . . ."

He picked it up from the desk.

Cuckoo had run quite a busy account over three or four years. First a loan, then a repayment, and, from time to time, a complete cancellation of the debt. Then, more. Never very much. The maximum was eighty pounds. At the time of Plaster's death, it had been fifty-six. Not much to murder Plaster for. All the same, if he hadn't been able to repay and Plaster had threatened to tell his employers and lose him his job. . . . It might have been Bastable. But all the time, according to Irma, there'd been quite a tidy sum in the Post Office in her name. It was fantastic.

" May I take the book, Mrs. Plaster? I'll see you get it back when I've had a good look at it."

" Take it with pleasure, if it'll help you. That's why I mentioned it. It may lead to somewhere. I'll confess I didn't care for Plaster. No use beating about the bush. People knew we weren't comfortable together. I might as well tell you than them do it and make it more unpleasant in the telling. Plaster was too mean and money-grubbing. He wasn't nice to know and he wasn't nice to me. I'm not surprised *The Bargees' Rest* lot gave him the cold shoulder. But when they give it to me, that's different. I was brought up decent and I'm as good as any of them are. They've no right to look down their noses at me. I own the property now, don't I? "

She was hurt about it. There were tears in her eyes.

"They were always glad to have me making them up at their shows. I've been a professional and I've forgotten more about the stage than they'll ever know. They're after me every time they put on a play. Then, when I turn up at *The Bargees' Rest*, they look at me as if the cat's brought me in. Well, they'll soon be out of their *Bargees' Rest* unless they mind their manners. . . ."

"Some of them are all right, though, aren't they?"

"Yes. Mr. Myers and Mr. Falconer are always perfect gentlemen to me. It's some of the women. That Irma. . . . Bastable's missus. Takes her all her time to speak to me. And her no better than she should be. I could tell you a thing or two about her ladyship's carryings-on at rehearsals. You'd be surprised. I see that no sooner is her poor husband in his grave, than she's off with another. . . . And a bright beauty he is, too."

"I don't want you to think I'm gossiping, Mrs. Plaster, because this is important. To whom are you referring when you speak about Mrs. Bastable's love affairs? Who, in particular, was involved?"

"The worst was with a man called Bradburn. I did hear he was a wealthy man, stockbroker, I think, in London. He was a prominent man in the dramatic society and although he was married, he fell hard for Irma. It was because she wouldn't leave him alone. I found them kissing in the dark corners when the lights were out. I don't know what happened, but Mr. Bradburn left the society for good and we never saw him again. Then, Mr. Carr at the bank had a spell. But that wasn't what you'd call dangerous or far-reaching, if you get what I mean. He was a decent young man and fell for Irma's charms. He used to take her home in his car. Then it stopped. She must have found someone else."

"Is that all?"

"I should think it was enough, Mr. Littlejohn. How many more do you want?"

"I want all the names of the men involved. Myers? Falconer?"

She was indignant.

"Certainly not. They're gentlemen. If they were anxious for that side of life . . . and I don't think for a minute they are . . . they'd aim higher than Irma Bastable. I wouldn't blame Mr. Falconer, mind you, if he did. The way his wife treats him."

"How?"

"Haven't you seen them together? She has him waiting on her hand and foot. He's never a minute to himself when she's around. And never a word of thanks. In fact, she'll criticize him openly in front of others. You'd think she'd married beneath her to hear her talk. Instead of which, he's far too good for her. No wonder he drinks more than he should. It 'ud drive any decent gentleman to the bottle."

It was getting time to go. Things had gone quite far enough.

"You'll keep all I've said about one and another of them to yourself, Superintendent, won't you? It would never do to get around."

"Of course. And thank you for your help, Mrs. Plaster."

"Don't mention it. And perhaps Mr. Falconer isn't as unhappy as we make out. He always seems cheerful enough. He's a sense of humour, which goes a long way. When the women at *The Bargees' Rest* are mentioned, though, it makes me see red the way some of them behave. I don't know how some of their husbands make ends meet. Specially that Irma. And Mrs. Falconer, too. The expensive taste she dresses in and she runs about in a car and. . . ."

They were at the door. It was past seven o'clock and Mrs. Plaster reversed the card again. CLOSED. Henry was due very shortly.

"How are you getting back?" she asked him as they said good-night.

"Taxi, I think."

"There's a place just round the corner. They're open."

Henry was struggling to put up the sun-blind of the health-stores as Littlejohn passed. The shop window was full of packets of herbs and all kinds of substitutes for meat and normal foods. A large advertisement in the middle of the window. *Dancer's Tonic for Lost Vitality.* Judging from Henry's struggles with the blind, he could have done with a course of his own medicine!

8

THE CLOWN

THE BASTABLE CASE spoiled Littlejohn's Sunday. It had turned out to be a commonplace, almost sordid affair, with nothing about it to get hold of and a dead-end at every turn.

Father Silvester had started it off with his tale about Alfie Batt and his conscience. It had all seemed quite simple. Bastable had an extravagant wife who had run him into debt. Probably he'd owed quite a number of shady little moneylenders like Plaster various sums. In fact, as much as they'd lend him. On occasions he found his wife carrying-on with some man or other. Then, instead of divorcing her or causing an unholy row, he went whining to the man, got money out of him, and, presumably, paid-off some of his more pressing creditors. Besides, banks don't like divorces among their staffs. An appearance in the courts, even as plaintiff, might have cost Bastable his job.

Then, Bastable found he couldn't borrow any more. So he started to dip into his till at the bank. Plaster began to press him for the comparatively small amount he owed him. Maybe they'd quarrelled and Bastable had hit him harder than he intended. He had disposed of the body in the canal, perhaps thinking Plaster quite dead.

A murder on his conscience as well as the shortage in his cash was a heavy burden for the defeated, whining little man, betrayed by his wife on top of it all. Then along came Alfie Batt with his blackmail. It was more than one man could stand. So he'd shot himself. And that was that. All nice and tidy.

And yet. . . .

The case was decidedly unpleasant. It had a taste of something crooked, some kind of jiggery-pokery. Someone knew more than they would tell.

There was Plaster with his little book of debts unpaid. Humpy, Cuckoo, Bimbo and Spider. . . . And the rest of them. What did they know about Plaster's fetching-up, dead, in the Waterbury Wharf?

It was Sunday morning and Littlejohn had been on Hampstead Heath for a walk with the dog. It was hot and oppressive and now there was thunder in the air. After lunch he felt irritable and he couldn't bear it any more. Somebody must be told about the murder of Plaster and the blackmailing of Bastable.

"Would you care for a run down to Brighton, Letty?"

His wife looked surprised.

"Not by road, on Sunday, Tom, please."

"By train, then?"

"If it will do you any good, I'll go with you. A breath of sea air might be a nice change."

He rang up Mrs. Utting's house in Chisholm Street, Brighton. Lulu answered cheerfully and talked to him like an old friend.

"I'm nearly dropping with the heat and the house is full of visitors. I'm run off my feet. Irma? She's not in . . . She went out for the day . . . Yes, I think I know where I might find her. You see, the roads are so congested that it's no pleasure motoring. So she said something about going to a party on the river near Shoreham. Mr. Peppercorn took her. . . ."

Littlejohn felt like saying that Peppercorn could damnwell bring her home again, but he didn't put it quite that way. It was urgent, he told Mrs. Utting, and he wished to see Irma right away. Perhaps Mr. Peppercorn would bring her back to Chisholm Street, but he was sorry that Peppercorn couldn't participate in the interview.

Then he ordered a taxi and he, Letty and the dog went to Victoria and caught the next train to Brighton. There, he left his wife and the dog sitting in a café on the promenade and went to Mrs. Utting's.

Irma was there waiting for him. Mrs. Plaster would have
said 'scandalous' again, if she'd seen her. She'd just returned
from the river party and was wearing a simple sun-dress
which had cost someone a pretty penny. It was in white
cotton satin, sprinkled with dark-blue dots which were perhaps a concession to mourning. It was held in position in a
mysterious way, for there were no shoulder-straps and it had
the intriguing feature of being ever ready to fall down to
the waist, but it never did.

Irma looked worried, but it did not deprive her of any
of her charms. In fact, it added to them by making her
appear rather helpless.

They met in a small room at the back, obviously Mrs.
Utting's private retreat. Judging from the noises emerging
from the lounge, some of the lodgers were watching tele-
vision.

"This is rather surprising, Superintendent."

Irma shook hands in the same clinging way. Mrs. Utting
was nowhere to be seen and a servant maid had let Littlejohn in.

"Mother's taking her Sunday nap. . . ."

"I'm sorry to disturb you, Mrs. Bastable, especially on
Sunday, but there are one or two things about your husband's death I think I ought to tell you. . . ."

He gave her a full account of what the teddy-boy had
confided to Father Silvester. The death of Plaster, the pur-
suit by Alfie Batt to Barnet, the blackmail, and the final
curtain.

As he told her the tale, Irma slowly appeared to grow
years older. Her body went limp, the sparkle left her eyes,
her face sagged, and she looked ready to faint. The attractive
summer frock began to seem pathetic.

"Are you sure? You're sure you've got the right man,
Superintendent?"

"A dying man was hardly likely to make up such a sen-
sational story. As for the right man, it all tallies with Barnet
and Moorgate, doesn't it? Are you ready to answer one or
two further questions? I didn't go fully into the matter

when last we met. I didn't want to distress you if we could clear up the mystery without it. But now, we seem up against a stone wall. You told me that you and your husband had some money saved. Why didn't he ask you for it and put his cash right, instead of shooting himself?"

Irma looked blankly round the room. An armchair, a few small cane chairs, a threadbare carpet, and a desk. And over the mantelpiece an enlarged snapshot of a man standing smiling, in front of an antique London taxi-cab. Presumably Utting himself. None of these seemed to give Irma any comfort. She began to weep. First slowly, then copiously.

"Had I better send for your mother?"

"No, please. I don't want to upset her. . . ."

She wiped her eyes and made an effort to compose herself. "If only I'd known. . . ."

And that was all she said for some time. Then she ceased her sobbing.

"If only you'd known what?"

"That he was short of money. I must have caused a mis-understanding when I told you about the savings when you were here before. They were in my name and I didn't tell my husband because he would have always been asking me for money. He was a bit reckless with money and tended to over-spend. . . ."

Reckless! That hardly seemed the word. Desperate was more like it. Desperately short of it.

"Let us get this straight, Mrs. Bastable. Your husband was not only wrong in his cash at the bank, but in debt to a moneylender. And yet, you are the only one who says he was a spendthrift. I think you told me something similar before. But only *you* have said it."

"Surely, I'm the one who would know!"

"What of his colleagues, his manager? None of them say that his way of life was extravagant. He'd not much money in his bank account when he died, but there were no signs in past drawings of irregular expenses, betting, gambling and such. In fact—forgive me if I'm brutal, but I must get at the truth—it is said that you lived above his income and were responsible for his money troubles."

She grew angry. It didn't improve her appearance. It made her look older and vulgar.

"Did the people at the bank tell you that? They were supposed to be our friends!"

"This was a police investigation, Mrs. Bastable, not an affair of backbiting and silly gossip."

"I didn't know my husband was in debt and I swear it. As I told you, he had very little expense in the way of clothes for me. Friends gave them to me."

"Surely, your husband would resent your receiving such gifts. Did he need to borrow to put up a show of supporting you decently?"

"He gave me a dress allowance."

"Could he afford it?"

"I don't know. He never discussed money with me."

"Was he still in love with you?"

She hesitated.

"Yes, I think he was."

"Did he ever object to your flirtations with other men?"

She looked dumbfounded, almost horror struck, but this time it was an act. She was fencing now to keep Littlejohn as much in the dark as she could.

"What do you mean?"

"What I say. Your flirtations, your affair with Bradburn —and your friendships with some of the men at the bank."

"You've learned quite a lot, Superintendent! And what, may I ask, is all this leading up to? To your accusing me of murdering my husband, perhaps. Well, let me tell you . . ."

"I said your husband had been seen carrying the body of Plaster to the canal and throwing it in. . . ."

"I don't believe it. He could never have carried Plaster, for a start. He was a puny, flabby man and quite incapable of carrying anybody. As for my affairs, as you call them, that is all lies and spiteful gossip wrung from people supposed to be my friends. That's all I have to say. And now, I must be going."

Littlejohn went on as though he hadn't heard.

"Did you know that your husband owed money to Plaster?"

"No. Why should he borrow from a little wretch like that? My husband despised him."

"But borrowed from him. Not very much, but enough to make him a bit afraid of Plaster. Your husband also borrowed from others."

"From who, may I ask?"

"From your lovers, Mrs. Bastable. He borrowed sums which he didn't repay from them."

Irma was looking less certain of herself. She couldn't guess just how much Littlejohn knew, and she was afraid.

"Why have you come to Brighton, Superintendent? To torture me, is it? What have you got against me?"

"Nothing. I want to know what might have impelled your husband to kill Plaster. And what made him steal a thousand pounds from his till. Can you help me? That's all."

She tore at her handkerchief and looked wild-eyed. The tears had washed away a lot of her make-up and left her bedraggled.

"I can't help you at all. . . ."

More tears.

"Do you think I might have a drink? There's whisky and a syphon in the cupboard under mother's desk."

Littlejohn found them. There were quite a lot of bottles, mainly gin, half of them empty. He mixed a drink.

"Please take one yourself, Superintendent. I'm sorry I flared-up, but I've been under a great strain of late."

He was glad to mix himself a stiff one, too. Dealing with a woman of temperament, in the true French sense, was a torment on a thundery day.

"May I go on?"

"Of course. . . ."

She was calmer again and sipped her drink eagerly. It did

her good and braced her. She even took out various articles
from her handbag and repaired the ravages of the tears. The
voluptuous huskiness returned to her voice.

"Before your husband died, did he seem to have money
to spare? In other words, if he'd robbed his till, did he
appear to have the cash on his person?"

"No, he did not. He still complained about having to pay
for things. I remember him asking me for ten shillings to
pay the plumber who'd called in the evening to put a new
washer on the tap. He said he'd just run short and would
repay me next day."

"So, in spite of his cash shortage, he was still hard-up. I
wonder what he did with the money."

"I don't believe he stole it at all. It was a mistake."

"A mistake? A thousand pounds is a lot of money. How
could it be a mistake?"

"A wrong entry in his books."

It all sounded very naïve. It was obvious that she didn't
believe Bastable had robbed his till, and was trying to find
a solution to the affair, however stupid.

"It isn't as easy as that, Mrs. Bastable. The books have
been checked. It was the cash which was wrong, not the
figures. We can take it the bank have satisfied themselves on
that score."

She gave him a blank stare. A very different Irma now
from the vital, disturbing woman who specialized in up-
setting the atmosphere at *The Bargees' Rest* and wherever
else she went.

"And why did he take his own life, if he wasn't in despair
because he couldn't put things right?"

"I don't know. Could someone else have shot him? That
might be it."

"No. He wasn't murdered. I've carefully examined the
records of the case. The wound had all the signs of self-
infliction. But it was the way he was holding the gun itself
which was most conclusive. It was grasped so hard in both
hands that the surgeon who examined the body had to force
it out. No murderer could have put it in the hands of his

D

victim so securely. We can almost be certain that he killed
himself."

" Almost? "

" If not, the situation was an incredible freak."

" Then he shot himself for some other reason. . . . Perhaps
his health. He hadn't been well."

" What ailed him? "

" His nerves were shot to pieces. He suffered from melan-
cholia all his life. He was like that when we first married.
It ran in his family, he once said. He used to get very
depressed."

Littlejohn paused thoughtfully.

" I think I ought to tell you, Mrs. Bastable, that we shall
have to re-open the whole case. It will involve a number of
further official enquiries. I'm afraid I shall have to question
among others, Mr. Bradburn."

" Oh. . . ."

She turned deadly pale. Littlejohn went and mixed her
another drink.

" Please don't . . . I beg you. It will bring out such a lot
of unhappiness which is better forgotten."

" Why . . . ? "

She drank half the whisky and soda and then rose to her
feet, her hands clasped.

" I beg you. . . . Please. . . ."

She was so used to putting on an act that even when she
was in earnest she couldn't help behaving like somebody on
the stage.

" You had better let me know why. And please sit down,
Mrs. Bastable. You'll feel far better if you relax. How long
is it since you lost touch with Bradburn? Please tell
the truth, because if you don't, Bradburn will probably
do so."

" Almost four years since. But you won't be able to see
him. He's been living in America since we parted. He went
and joined his brother there."

Parted! It gave you the impression of heavy dramatic
scenes, fond farewells, broken hearts. Probably Bradburn

had skedaddled and been glad to get away before Irma sucked him completely dry!

"You were his mistress?"

"We loved each other. . . ."

"Why did he go, then?"

"He was married and had three children. I told him it would be on my conscience if I was the cause of ruining two homes. . . . And especially spoiling the children's lives."

"Do you mind if I smoke my pipe?"

She seemed to awake from a daze and looked at the pipe in Littlejohn's hand and then at his pouch as though they were some kind of rare curiosities.

"I don't mind at all."

"So Bradburn went away. Were there others?"

"Superintendent! I'm not a loose woman! Of course there weren't others. If men like my company, it doesn't follow that I'm mistress of every one who takes me out to dinner."

"But your late husband might have thought so?"

"It is very unfair of you to insinuate that because of me he killed himself. He did no such thing. In fact, at the time he died, we'd thrashed the whole thing out and decided to start afresh."

"What had you thrashed out?"

It seemed a pity just as the climax of the drama was arriving, to prick the bubble by a stupid question, but it was the only way to keep Irma on the rails.

"My husband said I was too friendly with a certain man and that it had got to stop. I said it was only platonic and I could soon end it. He seemed so miserable that I got sorry and told him. . . ."

"You told him you'd send Carr about his business and behave yourself in future?"

Her eyes grew wide and her mouth opened. On her face was an expression which might have meant that Littlejohn was the man she'd long been seeking! A man who would tell her in plain terms the brutal truth!

"I never said it was Mr. Carr."

"But it was, wasn't it? And your husband objected to your intimacy with his colleagues. . . ."

"I told you, Superintendent, that I promised. . . ."

"And your husband accepted the promise and you both agreed to start afresh? He was happy?"

"He seemed so."

"So, it was hardly likely that he'd go almost at once and shoot himself?"

No reason why he shouldn't! A resumption of affectionate relations with Irma might have been more than Bastable could contemplate without going off his head altogether! However. . . .

"That's why I won't believe he shot himself out of unhappiness."

That, according to Irma dispensed with cash and melancholy as reasons for her husband's suicide. When Littlejohn asked her if she could suggest any other reason, she had to admit that she and Bastable weren't in the habit of confiding much in each other during the later years of their marriage.

"He kept his secrets to himself, if he had any. I did the same, because he didn't seem very interested."

"He never threatened to take his own life?"

"Never. Whenever he was depressed, his threat was always that he'd take to the road, like his father did."

"What did he mean by that?"

"His father was an eccentric, judging from what Cyril said, and didn't get on very well with his mother. Whenever things became intolerable between them, Cyril's father would take a rucksack and disappear and become a kind of tramp for months. Nobody knew where he'd gone. Then, one day, he'd turn up merry and bright and settle down again till next time."

"Did your late husband ever take to the road?"

"Of course not! He'd have got the sack from the bank. Cyril's father was a clergyman. It's easier for clergymen to be eccentric than bank clerks."

" Oh. I didn't know Mr. Bastable's father was a parson. Has he any relatives still living? "

" He has a sister who's a missionary in the south sea islands somewhere. I never met her. Cyril's father was a famous hymn-writer. . . ."

" Indeed. Did you ever meet him? "

" No."

Littlejohn almost asked if the Rev. Bastable wrote his hymns on the road, but things had taken an unexpected turn into uselessness. This wasn't the way to solve the Bastable case!

" Did you call one another nicknames at the dramatic society? "

" Sometimes. We were very familiar with one another, you see. You know how things get when you're nearing a show. All keyed-up and affectionate. Then when it's over, it all flops. At the affectionate stage we called one another pet names."

Littlejohn could imagine it. Familiarity and affection, and then somebody kissing Irma in the wings, as Mrs. Plaster had said. He looked at Irma. She was her vital seductive self again, her poise regained.

" Did you ever call anybody by the nickname of Bimbo? "

" Bimbo? I don't remember it. Why? "

" Because Plaster had a little book of names for his borrowers. He was a moneylender as well as other things. . . ."

Littlejohn recited the list. Humpy, Carrot, Red, Bimbo, Cuckoo. . . .

" Does any name strike a chord? "

" Cuckoo! That's a strange one."

Poor old Bastable!

She confessed that although they were queer and reminded her of a children's play, none of them conveyed anything to her.

To Littlejohn, the names were just as fantastic as the case. A lot of stupid suffocating details and not a single clue.

Outside, someone was blowing the horn of a car.

" That'll be Leslie Peppercorn. He said he'd come and take me back to Shoreham when I was ready. Will there be anything more, Superintendent? "

Irma was indeed herself again and she and Littlejohn were going to part on good terms. Perhaps she was thinking that next time *he'd* start to call her by a pet name. Or again, perhaps she thought she'd come very well out of the interview.

" You'll regard what I've told you as confidential, Superintendent? "

" I'll treat it with great discretion."

" Thank you. I'll give your kind regards to mother. . . ."

He was one of the family already!

" . . . and if that's all, I'll just go and tidy-up before I leave. Bimbo. . . ."

She paused.

" It seems familiar, but it evades me. I'll think of it when I'm not trying and then I'll let you know. Give me your 'phone number."

Another blast of the motor-horn. It seemed to inspire Irma.

" I think I've remembered. It was years ago at the dramatic society. We gave a poor children's party and we ran a circus to amuse them afterwards. It was Christmas, you see. We couldn't have real animals, so we made them. Pantomime horses and cows, cats, dogs and rabbits. I was a rabbit. . . ."

Littlejohn could see it. Bastable in the hindquarters of a stage horse and Falconer in the front capering heavily round and crossing their legs when they halted. And, of course, Irma as a pretty little rabbit, exuding the latest perfume from Paris.

" We had two clowns, too, to crack jokes and pour water down each other's trousers. It was a great success. One was the funny man and the other was the stooge."

She was completely carried away by her recollections.

" What about Bimbo? "

" That was one of the clowns. Bimbo and Bobo. Cyril was Bobo, I remember. The only part he ever took, and it was a huge success. Bimbo whitewashed him from head to foot and then emptied what was left in the bucket over him. The children went mad with delight. . . ."

Littlejohn could imagine poor old melancholy Bastable, the defeated one, suffering under the whitewash whilst the pretty little rabbit canoodled somewhere in the scenery out of sight!

"Who was Bimbo?"

Littlejohn could hardly wait. Outside, the horn was blowing again.

"Alec Falconer. He makes a lovely clown, you know."

That was it! A lovely clown! Red nose, gangling shuffle, desolate, bored expression. . . .

"May I go now? I'll see you again soon, I hope."

He bade her good-bye and she gave his hand a long affectionate squeeze.

"I can't tell you how grateful I am, in all this unhappiness, for your kindness, Superintendent. I know I can depend on you to look after me."

When the Superintendent reached the door he found a policeman booking Peppercorn for obstruction. The enormous car seemed to fill the little street. Peppercorn didn't seem to mind. It was all part of his overheads in winning the favours of Irma.

Littlejohn was glad to see his wife and the dog and they were certainly glad to see him.

"Everything all right, and was it worth the trip?" asked his wife.

"Yes. Well worth it. . . ."

Littlejohn wondered why he felt so melancholy in spite of it.

9

MONDAY EVENING

THE LITTLEJOHNS ARRIVED back home by seven o'clock, at which time Cromwell turned-up to supper. He was flushed with success, for he had just finished decorating his flat. All that remained now was to clean the stray paint from clothes, furniture, carpets and fittings and then he could join his family in Cornwall for holidays.

After the meal, Littlejohn and Cromwell smoked over glasses of cool beer. Outside it was still sunny and fine, but the evening had grown airless and muggy as though another thunderstorm were on the way.

Cromwell was puzzled that Littlejohn should be so concerned with a case which had already closed to the satisfaction of two coroners.

Bastable had committed suicide. There had been a verdict to that effect. The experts had testified to a bullet, obviously self-inflicted, in the heart, from a revolver so savagely clutched in the dead man's *two* hands, that they'd had great difficulty in releasing it. It certainly could not have been put there by a murderer after death.

" So, he committed suicide, old chap. He was wrong in his cash—an excellent motive for a neurotic like Bastable—as well as worried by his wife's infidelities and extravagance, and by the levies of the young blackmailer. In addition, he'd drowned another tormentor in the canal. Any one of those was a reason for suicide."

" And yet, you aren't satisfied? "

" No. What happened to the thousand pounds he'd taken from his till? From all accounts, Bastable had gone through it between the official surprise check less than a month before his death, and the time he shot himself. He owed a paltry

104

sum to Plaster. Why should he want to murder him? Surely not for that. Had Plaster been blackmailing him, too? If so, for what? And on top of it all, Bastable was a puny, flabby, cowardly chap, out of condition, who'd have been horrified at the very thought of killing anybody. Although, some murderers we've known were equally ineffective and incompetent and yet managed to remove their victims. But I can't rest until I've got it all tidy in my mind."

"Shall I put off my holidays and give you a hand, sir?"

It was said with such earnestness and devotion that Littlejohn's heart warmed to his sergeant.

"Of course not, old man. It's good of you to offer, but this is just a little matter of my own I've got to settle properly. I won't hear of you staying behind. . . . And now let's forget it and have some more beer."

Telephone. It was Myers.

"I've been trying to get you most of the day, Superintendent. You forgot the whisky bottle in Bastable's locker when you left last night."

It was ten o'clock. No time to do anything now.

"Thank you, sir. There were a number of men in the room when I went and, as you know, I'm anxious not to cause any alarm at *The Bargees' Rest*. To have taken it away under their noses yesterday would have been rather spectacular."

"I've kept it locked-up all day, and the cupboard hasn't even been opened since you saw the bottle."

"Perhaps I could call round tomorrow, then. Will you be there in the evening?"

"I'll be going straight from the office. On Monday night, we tidy up after the week-end's orgies."

"Shall we meet then? I'll be at Scotland Yard about six. If you could call for me there, we could have a snack together and then go out to the canal in a police car."

Myers jumped at it. Quite an experience and something to boast about to his colleagues.

". . . When I was dining with Littlejohn at Scotland Yard. . . ."

D*

" Six, then? "

" Right. And thanks for the trouble, Mr. Myers."

Next evening Myers was at Scotland Yard before time. They ate sandwiches and drank beer in Littlejohn's room and at six-thirty they were away, Littlejohn driving.

Monday night was mechanics' night at *The Bargees' Rest*, too. A quarter of a mile down the towpath was a basin with a warehouse behind, and this had been converted into a boat-house and dock for the club. There were at least forty boats of all kinds tied-up there; some had been hauled on a tongue of land which had formerly held loading cranes. There was a little white-painted jetty and an old spring-board for those who cared to bathe in the glaucous water. It had belonged to a swimming club which had long been defunct. No wonder!

About half-a-dozen men were busy tinkering with the engines or on the overturned bodies of little craft.

Myers showed Littlejohn round and introduced him to several of the members he hadn't already met. Most of them, immersed in the innards of motors, were too busy to be sociable.

Then, Littlejohn and Myers walked along the path to *The Bargees' Rest*. There were half-a-dozen cars parked behind the old inn, and two or three groups of people sitting around, enjoying the cool of the evening and drinking beer. A few patient fishermen festooned the edge of the water, hating the passing craft gliding lazily by because they disturbed the fish. A couple of boats moored to the side; their owners had stopped for a drink.

A man passed in a green rowing-boat loaded with fishing tackle. He looked worried, as though his task were an arduous one.

Myers walked here and there, examining the building, the paintwork, the inside and outside. He took his duties as secretary seriously. He complained about the general untidiness of members who had left articles of clothing, cigarette ends, matches and waste paper about the dressing-rooms.

" I'll put a notice on the board. It's not good enough."

A man, obviously a part-time steward, started to sweep-out the locker-rooms. The lounge, where the teas were served on busy days, had been tidied, and the floor of composition tiles mopped clean. There was nobody about, with the exception of those outside and the servant at his task.

"Shall we sit in here and have a talk before we go?"

Myers frowned. He was so fond of his honorary job, that he couldn't bear to be idle when he was on the premises. He had just opened the garbage-bin in the kitchen and found it hadn't been emptied.

"You'll see to this dust-bin, Sam?" he shouted at the steward, who pretended not to hear.

"Sam!!"

"I 'eard yer. The dust-cart'll call tomorrer. I'll leave it out for 'em. It'll cost you another half-dollar. It's off the reg'lar beat 'ere."

Myers came in the lounge with two bottles of beer from the refrigerator, and opened them.

"Good health."

"Here's to you."

Myers looked at Littlejohn in a questioning way, inviting him to open the ball.

"Can you give me a bit of background about Bastable, Mr. Myers? I mean, where he came from, his career, and his way of life."

Myers put down his glass.

"Is there something more than you've already told us about Bastable's death, sir? It surely wasn't murder, but by the way you're investigating it, one would think so."

Littlejohn told him about the teddy-boy, Plaster's death, the blackmail, and Bastable's share in it all.

Myers was dumbfounded. He just couldn't believe it. He took a cigarette mechanically from a packet, forgot to light it, and sat there with it dangling from his nether lip.

"Bastable wouldn't murder anybody. There must have been some mistake or else somebody's lying. He was too much of a weakling and a coward."

"That's no alibi, sir. Half the convicted murderers are

just that type. Unlikely little people, baited beyond endurance or driven to despair by circumstances, who finally
eliminate the obstacle to their safety or to what they believe to be their happiness."

"But Bastable . . . I knew him. He was a friend. . . ."

"How long?"

"Ever since he entered the bank. He came from Barnet
and I was born in South Mimms. We were in the same bank
from the start. As juniors, we travelled to work together
and we often spent our spare time together, too. Bastable,
a murderer? It's nonsense!"

"He owed money to Plaster, and Plaster may have threatened him. Bastable may have struck him hard in a fit of
temper."

"He never had a temper. He was a coward, really. He
hated pain or quarrelling of any kind. He'd go to any extent
for a bit of peace. He was never robust. During the war
they put him in the Pay Corps. He was stationed somewhere
in Lancashire all the time."

"What made him so hard-up?"

"His wife. I remember his meeting her. He was on relief
at Brighton for six months one summer, and she was the
landlady's daughter. . . ."

It sounded like an old comic song!

". . . He fell hard for her. No wonder. He'd never had
much to do with girls before. Too timid. Irma was on the
spot, recovering from an illness. She taught him all he'd
missed in the past. She encouraged him. He was never her
sort, at all. She was a passionate, I almost said, predatory
woman, and so damned attractive that men couldn't leave
her alone. She's still that way, at forty, too."

It was said in short, breathless sentences, as though he
were having to force the information reluctantly out.

"How old was he, then?"

"Twenty-seven, about. I can tell from my own age."

"And Irma would be . . . ?"

"Seventeen. There were ten years between them."

"A mere girl?"

"By age only. She was a full-grown woman in every other way. She'd been through dramatic school and was in a rep. company when Bastable met her."

"What happened during the war when Bastable was away in Lancashire?"

"She was with a party entertaining the troops. She even went to Cairo."

"I see. Funny, after all that, she and Bastable ever came together again."

"Yes, isn't it? But they did, for some reason. I think Bastable begged her to come back. Those parties of entertainers fell apart when the war ended, you know. She was at a loose end and had been ill again. With Bastable she'd at least a home and food and clothes to depend upon."

"Did Bastable still love her when he died, do you think?"

Myers looked embarrassed. He wasn't a sentimental man at all. Sentiment made him feel awkward. Give him some figures to unravel, or a club or an office to organize and he was in his element. But ask him about emotions and he was at sea.

"As a matter of fact, he was mad about Irma all his life. I don't know how he stood it. He knew about the other men and yet, he took it lying down because he hadn't the guts or the spirit to kick up a fuss and he was afraid he'd lose Irma if he did. He told me so a time or two."

"When he was trying to borrow money from you?"

Another pause. Littlejohn couldn't help admiring Myers. He was loyal to his friends. He hadn't much imagination, but he stuck to his guns about Bastable. Even if he had robbed the bank, they'd been friends.

"He asked me a time or two. But I could hardly make ends meet myself. We got poorly paid in those days and I'd more to do with my money than lend it to Bastable to help him buy Irma what other men would give her if Bastable didn't. I'd the wife and kids to keep and a mortgage on the house to pay-off."

"So, he borrowed elsewhere?"

"He must have done. I can only think he robbed his till to meet his debts. Though who he owed all that money to, I couldn't even guess."

"Did he ever threaten suicide when you wouldn't help him?"

"Never. He whined and even wept, but he never threatened to kill himself. You'd have thought he'd have done that when she was having the affair with Bradburn. That was the limit. He'd grounds for a divorce there if ever he had. And yet, he forgave her and took her back. She went off to live with her mother for several weeks whilst that was going on."

Littlejohn lit his pipe and Myers went off and returned with more beer. Outside, it was completely quiet. The men at the tables on the terrace were silently smoking and drinking, just enjoying the peace. Whenever a boat passed the engine broke the stillness and gradually died away in the distance and they could hear the water of the backwash gently lapping against the banks.

"What did Irma see in Bastable at the start?"

"She was seventeen and she'd been ill. Bastable had money and I believe he treated her like a queen. Her mother once told me that he spent money on her like water when she was convalescent."

"He'd money, you say?"

"His mother, a widow, had just died and left him what she had. His father had been a parson, who was knocked down by a steam-roller and killed. He used to ride a tricycle about his parish when he was in it. He was an eccentric, who used to disappear from circulation for months at a time. He'd pack a rucksack and vanish. Once, they found him, after three months, in a retreat where he'd been praying and meditating; and once they brought him back from London where he'd spent a month living with a prostitute he said he'd reformed. They hushed it up. He often became a sort of tramp, too, sleeping in lodging-houses among publicans and sinners, as he called them. Bastable told me all this when we were pals in the old days. Well, the old chap eventually pedalled round a corner right into a traction-engine. And that ended it."

Bastable had certainly got entangled with a rum lot of relatives and in-laws. Falling in the fire, cannoning into steam-rollers. . . . Myers was still talking. He'd brought on yet another lot of beer.

". . . His mother always stuck to the old man whatever his latest scandal happened to be. It must have run in the family. Bastable was the same, the way he stuck to Irma."

Myers brooded over his beer and then drank three quarters of a glassful in one gulp, as though he, too, had decided to end it all in despair. He solemnly wobbled off for two more.

"It's a hot and thirsty night," he said.

"You were saying Bastable had come into his mother's money. . . ."

"Yes. It was about £5,000. They got damages out of the local corporation. The steam-roller was on its wrong side. Bastable didn't tell Irma how much he had. He told me so himself. Once when he was pleading poverty to me. He cried. Irma thought he was very well-off, you see. Otherwise, I'm sure she'd never have married him. His mother was a daughter of an archdeacon and doctor of divinity, and I guess Irma thought Bastable's family were bishops or something. She as good as said so to my wife, once. She was trying to justify her conduct and prove that Bastable had deceived her. . . . Where was I?"

He looked fuddled. Ready to have a good cry himself about the tragic irony of life.

"Bastable and Irma painted Brighton red when she was fit to get around again. They got married, too. Bastable confessed it to me once when he'd had too much to drink and was in one of his moods, that she forced him into it. Said there was a child on the way. He always believed there'd been a mishap about that child, but I never did. No. I did not. She just tricked him. That's my view. Tricked him. Then, it turned out that all ma's money was spent. That was when Irma started to go off the rails. That and the war did it. Her revenge. . . ."

Myers paused. He seemed surprised to find himself talking so glibly. He looked at his empty glass again and at Little-john's full one. Then he shook his head.

"I oughtn't to be telling you all this. I was Bastable's friend. But if I don't tell you, someone else will and they won't hold Bastable's end up like I will. I liked Bastable, in spite of his foolish, spineless way. He'd his good points and I challenge anybody to say he hadn't."

He looked aggressively at Littlejohn, as though the Super-intendent were going to take up the gauntlet.

"He shot himself, and I don't somehow blame him. If he took the bank cash, I don't blame him, either. Plenty more where that came from, isn't there? Irma sucked every cent and more out of him, and from a sort of innocent and stupid, but likeable young feller, she made a mug of him. What do you expect? He was a parson's son and his mother was a parson's daughter. There were rural deans in the family and D.D.s, and I wouldn't be surprised if there wasn't a bishop or two. . . . He'd been brought up soft. Religion's that way. It makes a lot of people strong; but a few it makes soft. Bastable was one of the softies. Irma made him even worse than that. She turned him into a defeated, cringing little nobody that everybody would have given the cold shoulder to, if Irma hadn't been so damned attractive. When he shot himself, he went without any hope or faith left. . . ."

And Myers burst into tears.

If Bastable thought he hadn't a friend in the world when he killed himself, he'd been mistaken!

Myers awkwardly composed himself.

"Excuse me. I've drunk too much. But I want you to know one thing. I don't believe Bastable took the cash. I was there when his books and cash were checked and he *was* wrong. Figures such as we deal with in banks don't lie. He was a thousand wrong. But I don't believe it. You'll think I'm mad. But I don't. He never stole a thing in his life and he'd had a pretty raw and rough time. All through it, he was never dishonest."

"Perhaps that's why he killed himself. He'd broken his principle."

"No."

Myers took on a stubborn look and seemed ready to argue until doomsday about it.

"What about Bradburn? What happened?"

Myers looked hard at Littlejohn.

"You know a lot, don't you? And you're still not satisfied. Look! Are you beginning to believe me when I say Bastable didn't pinch the cash?"

"I don't know; but I'm going to find out."

Myers stretched out his hand.

"Shake. You're a good sort. At first, I thought you were just another nosey cop. Now, I think you're a gentleman. Shake again."

Outside it was growing dusk. The men on the terrace kept peeping-in wondering what Myers and Littlejohn were doing. Finally, they began to break-up and you could hear them shunting their cars about at the back of the club-house and leaving for home.

"Bradburn? Yes. He and Irma played opposite each other in one or two plays at the dramatic society. Love scenes. They got going about together. That's how it always happened. The play became the real thing. Irma was a menace. As I said, it looked that time as if there'd be a divorce. But Bradburn's wife must have written to her brother, who arrived from Canada. He was a tycoon; a huge chap who'd made his money in wood . . . in lumber. He soon showed the weight of his money. He carried Bradburn off and his wife and family with him. One day Bradburn was there; the next, he'd vanished. He left Irma a note which took the wind out of her sails for a bit. She soon recovered, but it taught her a lesson. She was careful after that. Flirtations were all that could be laid at her door. What went on on the q.t., I wouldn't like to guess."

"What about Plaster?"

"What about him?"

"Did he attend rehearsals regularly?"

"More or less. He scene-painted and we paid him for it. We also hired furniture and a lot of properties from him. He was always hanging around. He'd been connected with the stage one time in his life and our society seemed to attract him. We didn't encourage him, because occasionally he'd arrive the worse for drink and get a bit offensive with the ladies. But he was useful, you see. Scene-shifting, making properties. . . . He even had a good working knowledge of stage lighting."

"Did he ever lend money to the members?"

Myers looked sharply at Littlejohn. He wondered where all the information had come from.

"Yes, he did. He started by offering to lend one of our fellows money to buy a car. After that, I'm sure one or two did get loans from him on the sly."

"Any bank men?"

Myers was horrified.

"Good Lord, no! It's forbidden by the staff regulations."

"So, Bastable. . . ."

Myers didn't give him time to finish.

"I'm sure he didn't."

"Yet, Bastable, according to Alfie Batt, the teddy-boy, threw Plaster's body in the canal. Why should he have knocked Plaster out and done such a thing?"

"It beats me. I don't believe it. In the first place, as I've told you before, he hadn't the stamina for the physical effort or the guts to hit or murder anybody."

"Bastable was seen giving money to Plaster here, behind the club. I'd think he was repaying a loan."

"He was running a terrible risk. He'd have been for the high-jump if the bank had got to know. Plaster was a good customer of the bank. . . ."

"You mean at Moorgate?"

"Yes. Our manager, Mr. Abbott, sometimes attended rehearsals at the dramatic society. He's interested in the social side of the staff as well as their work at the office. Plaster took a fancy to Mr. Abbott. He said he was a perfect gentleman, which is true. He insisted on transferring his account from the London and Southern Bank at Barnet to our office. When he did so, Abbott got the shock of his life. It was quite a big account. Plaster did good business in antiques in the West End and had a large turnover. The account was worth having, I can tell you."

"Perhaps Plaster threatened to tell the bank about Bastable's borrowing from him and Bastable lost his temper and hit him."

"Were there signs of violence on Plaster's body when it was taken from the water?"

"No. But there are ways of knocking-out a man without leaving bruises or other traces."

"But how could Bastable know all that? He was no fighter or gymnast. He was in the Pay Corps in the war, not in the Commandos. . . ."

"By the way, it's getting dark and it's almost ten. We ought to go, Mr. Myers. But, before we do, let me give you a word of friendly advice. If you're thinking of buying this place, you'd all better be much nicer to Mrs. Plaster. She's got the huff with some of you for giving her the cold-shoulder. She's thinking of turning you out. This is a hint in case you want to get the *Rest* at a reasonable price."

Myers looked dumbfounded.

"Thanks for the tip, sir. I'll not forget," he said sheepishly.

"Just one more matter before we part, Mr. Myers. Has Bastable ever been wrong in his cash before?"

"An odd pound or two. Anybody might be that. It's quite a regular thing at a busy counter, you know."

"How often is the cash checked?"

"Monthly by the management. Quarterly, as a rule, by the visiting inspectors. It's always what we call a *surprise* check."

"When was the cash checked last before Bastable's death?"

"Almost a month before. Mr. Abbott, Mr. Carr and myself checked all the tills. Mr. Abbott did the chief cashier's, which is the largest amount and is Falconer's. Mr. Carr checked Bastable's till. It was right to a penny."

" Mr. Carr, eh? "

" Yes. Why? "

" He's one of Irma's admirers, I believe."

" Yes, but there's no harm in Carr. It's only a mild flirtation."

" I believe Carr didn't like Bastable."

" He said he was a slacker, that's all."

" So, in less than a month, Bastable took a thousand pounds? "

" He must have done, if you admit he was a thief. I've heard of cashiers evading managers' and inspectors' checks by smart tricks, but Bastable was too slow and mentally heavy to pull-off such a thing."

" Are you sure? "

" Dead sure. I've known him all my life. He was absolutely incapable of breaking the system of cash checking."

" And yet he was wrong less than a month after."

" Yes. Next time his till was checked it was sure to be found out, too."

" And that's why he shot himself? "

" I can only think that's the reason. But why did he need the cash? What did he do with it? "

What? That was the mystery.

" What about Falconer? "

" What do you mean? "

" He's a rum card, isn't he? How long's he been in London? "

" Six or seven years."

" He lives near you? "

" Yes, Barnet. A few minutes away by car."

" I heard you and the Bastables were very good to Falconer and his wife when they came south."

" I was in the old Moorgate branch then. So was Bastable. We took the Falconers under our wing. In fact, the Falconers stayed for a few nights with the Bastables till they found rooms. We've no accommodation ourselves with the kids. We helped them get a house in the neighbourhood and we all became friends."

" Was Falconer always like he is now? "

" He was quite a good-looking chap till he went bald and too much drink flushed his face and nose. He was always casual. Never seemed keen to get on. Listless. No *go*."

" Have you ever guessed why? "

"Temperament, for one thing. He's quite a clever chap, you know. Literary. A big reader. But would you believe it, he told me quite recently he only reads one book now? It's in twelve volumes and when he's got to the twelfth, he starts at number one and goes all through again. Sort of perpetual motion. I think it's an author called Proust. A Frenchman. Falconer knows French like a native. He was in the Resistance over there during the war and I believe was parachuted there a time or two. . . . Where were we? "

It was getting late and there wasn't another soul about. Outside, the sunset had given place to a kind of dark green twilight. They could just see the darker masses of the low hills downstream. Across the canal, the lighted windows of houses shimmered through the last of the dusk. Myers switched on the light.

"Another beer before we go, Superintendent? "

" I think not, sir. I've had enough."

Myers had recovered from his drinks of strong export lager and there was no sense in fuddling him again.

" We were talking about Falconer and his reading Proust. And why he's so lackadaisical. . . ."

Myers had grown confidential in the quiet night.

" I must say, between ourselves, his wife's never encouraged him. He'd have been better for a little pushing from her. Fleur is a lovely-looking woman. Don't you agree? Never seems to get any older. In more ways than one, too. Her looks don't change or spoil. Neither does her mind. You'd think that living with a cultivated, fastidious fellow like Falconer, would have taught her something. Instead, she's never grown-up. She's still like somebody in a girls' school. The world's passed her by and left her innocent and unaffected. She keeps Falconer constantly on the move waiting on her. She's very stand-offish if she doesn't take to anyone and that's kept them short of friends. Falconer's lonely, you know. And bored. That's why he drinks; and Fleur doesn't seem to mind him doing it. But he never complains. He seems to have some inner strength in him that keeps him invulnerable and good-tempered, although he's a cynic right to the core. He says some funny things. Know what he said on Saturday night to me . . . ? "

Myers paused and looked ready to surprise Littlejohn.

"We'd been talking about Irma after she and Peppercorn had gone. And *à propos* of nothing at all, Falconer comes out with the strangest thing. 'We don't love women for what they are,' he says, 'But for what we make them. We endow them with all the characteristics we'd like them to have, and we fall in love with the creature we create.' Damn' silly, I call it. I'd quite an argument, you might almost call it a row, with my wife when we got home, about it. It seemed to upset her properly."

"It's Marcel Proust, you know. . . ."

"Not the fellow who wrote the dozen volumes! Well, I'll be damned!"

Littlejohn rose and spoke casually.

"Did Irma ever make a pass at Falconer?"

Myers looked anywhere but at Littlejohn.

"Well . . . yes she did. As I told you, the Falconers stayed with the Bastables for a bit. Then they went in rooms till they found a house. I never heard of any real affair going on, but both me and my wife intercepted queer looks between Irma and Falconer sometimes in those days. Falconer, of course, was imperturbable. He'd never roll his eyes at a woman in public. Or tête à tête, for that matter. But Irma can never hide her feelings. Those intimate, secret looks you sometimes see between lovers. I suppose there was nothing in it. We were relieved when it fizzled out."

"Has Mr. Abbott, your manager, a soft spot for Irma, too? I know it's a bit nauseating doing the rounds about Irma, but. . . ."

"You thinking of the way he defended her when you hinted she might be a spendthrift?"

You hinted! Littlejohn smiled. That was a good one! When all of them had been hard at it accusing Irma of ruining Bastable!

" Yes."

" That's his way. He's really a first-rate fellow and a perfect gentleman. Considerate to the staff, interested in their families and well-being. Gives us all a party every winter. He only tried to protect Irma because he was sorry about all the trouble she had. There's no question of anything else. He's happily married to a lovely wife, has two fine boys, and he wouldn't look at another woman."

Myers began to look uneasy.

" I don't know what my wife will say. I'm not usually so late. She'll think I've fallen in the canal. I'll just ring her up. . . ."

He wasn't long about it.

" I'd better take a look round and then lock-up. Is there anything more, Superintendent? I must say we've had a long session together and I hope you'll regard what I've said as confidential. It's been a pleasure to have your company and I do hope you'll come again."

" I think that will be all, sir, and thanks for your great help and hospitality. I'll treat all you've said with great discretion."

Discretion! Blessed word! Myers glowed at the sound of it.

They walked round the clubhouse together and Myers tried the doors and fastened the windows.

" Could a smart man continue wrong in his cash for months, in spite of periodic surprise checks by independent officials? "

Myers stood still and nodded firmly.

" Yes. I've known it done. But it's bound to come out one day and it needs a clever man to keep it up any length of time."

" Will you explain to me how it's done sometime? "

Myers was definitely embarrassed now. It was one of those banking secrets best forgotten.

"I'd rather you saw one of the higher officials about that, Superintendent. You see, it wouldn't do. . . . But then you're police, aren't you? You could, more or less, force the issue, couldn't you?"

"No, Mr. Myers. I wouldn't for the world make things awkward for you. Leave it, and I'll have a word with some of my colleagues in the Fraud Squad. They know all the tricks of the trade. Meanwhile, you can do one thing for me, as accountant of your branch. Will you please take a look round and see if Bastable or anyone else showed signs of using the system you mention recently?"

"You mean, you persist in thinking that Bastable might have tried it on, after all?"

"Yes, he might. He might have come across it somewhere in his career."

Myers shook his head slowly and then put his hat on it.

"I doubt it. He was too nervous and ham-handed."

"If you do find anything, please let me know right away, before you mention it to anyone, and you and I will see Mr. Abbott together about it."

"Very well, Superintendent. By the way, what about the whisky bottle? We almost forgot it again."

They went together to the locker room, which was in darkness. Myers put on the lights, took out his duplicate keys, and opened Bastable's locker.

The whisky bottle wasn't there.

10

AN EVENING WITH CHRISTINE

SHORTLY BEFORE SIX o'clock the next evening, the huge black figure of Father Silvester crossed the embankment to Scotland Yard. His companion was again Christine Bobbitt. This time, she had, presumably under instructions, abandoned her matadors and wore, instead, a short red cotton skirt, which spread like a miniature crinoline round her knees, and a yellow, sleeved knitted jumper. She would have preferred to show more of herself, but the priest had told her approximately what to wear and prohibited her exotic make-up of mascara and scented powder, in place of which she had daubed her mouth with an extra thick layer of lipstick which didn't match her clothes. She trotted resentfully at the priest's side, trying to keep up with his long strides, the stiletto steel heels of her white shoes tapping like a typewriter on the pavement.

Littlejohn was waiting in a police car in the yard. He had decided that it might be a good thing to go over the ground covered by Alfie Batt and his girl on their scooter on the fateful night in May.

At the sight of the car, the sulk left Christine's face and she gave a shrill staccato laugh.

"It's too small. You'll need a shoe-horn to get him in it."

The priest proved her wrong by easing his huge bulk in the back seat. The springs twanged and clanked and the back of the car sank.

"Get in there beside the Superintendent and behave yourself!"

Christine took it all mildly. She was either scared or very fond of the priest who, in his younger days, had once given her father a good hiding for beating-up her mother.

"What's the idea? I've a date at seven. Where are we goin'?" she said to Littlejohn, who patiently explained.

"I want to cover the route you and Alfie Batt went over on the night you went to Waterbury Wharf."

"It'll take too long. Ernie'll be waitin' for me and he'll get mad. An' when Ernie gets mad. . . ."

"Be quiet! You can see Ernie another time, and if he looks like getting cross when you meet, tell him I want a word with him."

Father Silvester then moved himself into a more comfortable position, heaved the car up and down, crossed his hands over his stomach, and told Littlejohn to get going. Christine gazed stonily through the window. There was no fun in a night out with what she later described as a couple of squares.

"I want you, if you can, Christine, to tell me the road you took to Waterbury Wharf."

Christine turned a disgusted face to Littlejohn. Her bottom lip had grown to twice its normal thickness.

"How should I know? I was on the back of the scooter, holdin' on for dear life. I'd no time for seein' the sights on the way."

Then she began to hum a dismal beat tune to which she writhed her shoulders and twisted her feet in convulsions. She took a cigarette from her bag and jammed it in her lips. Father Silvester snatched it out and threw it through the window.

"I said behave yourself."

Golder's Green, Edgware, Watford. . . .

The roads were comparatively quiet. Everyone seemed to have turned-in to tea and the full rush of evening hadn't yet begun. Buses half-empty, shops closed, people in groups here and there talking in desultory fashion. Twilight was beginning to set-in over London after another sizzling day.

At Maida Vale they passed a belated barrow-boy known to Christine, who hung out of the window and screamed something incoherent to him. Then she resumed her dull chant of despair.

The colours of things were less intense and passers-by looked relaxed and heavy-limbed. Many of the men were without coats and the women in light summer frocks. Now and then, a sun-frock passed or a straw hat. The crowds thinned-out as the car left the inner suburbs behind and soon they could see the distant wooded hills ahead with the sun hanging over them like a red ball of fire.

Littlejohn had studied the large scale-map and knew exactly where he was going. Between King's Langley and Berkhampstead he turned left into a side-road. The next turn to the right brought them to a sunken track of broken asphalt, with large potholes from which the water had dried in the drought, leaving a hard cake of filthy mud instead. There were traces, from the impression of car tyres, that the road was well used. Littlejohn stopped the car in a gateway beyond which was open country dotted here and there with clumps of new property and, now and then, a large house in a garden.

" Have you been here before, Christine? "

She was now chewing gum and looked as if, had she been a cat, she would have purred. Instead, she levered herself up on the seat, looked out unintelligently, and then nodded.

"Yep! It's near where Alfie parked the scooter the second time we come out here. The night we came to *The Boatmen's Rest.*"

" *The Bargees' Rest. . . .* "

"You know where I mean. Yes. There's another gate jest down the lane. That's where Alfie left me. If he thought I'd stay parked there, he'd another think comin'. I went down the lane. . . ."

" We'll do the same. Tell us where you parked, Christine."

Littlejohn put the car in bottom gear and slowly moved along.

" Here."

Another halt and they all got out. At first she didn't fancy it.

" I'm very cosy here now. I'll wait till you both come back."

Father Silvester opened the front door on Christine's side.

"Come along. You'll get in mischief if we leave you. . . ."

"When do we eat? I haven't had anythin' solid since four o'clock."

Littlejohn tapped her gently on the shoulder.

"When we've finished our business, you shall have anything you like to order, Christine."

They hadn't far to go before the roof of *The Bargees' Rest* came in sight. They were on the old draymen's road and round the corner was obviously the large cutting which held the old watermen's inn. They halted.

"Better not let ourselves be seen. My spying round the place might cause a panic. They've already got wind at *The Bargees' Rest* that there's something fishy about Bastable's death. Now, Christine. What did Alfie do when he came down here?"

"I watched him get through the hedge and climb the hill there. . . ."

The gap in the hedge was there and the hill was the embankment behind the inn, thrown up, probably, when it was built, from the soil and rubble excavated from the cutting.

"Let's all get through the hedge and then we'll be out of sight if any more visitors come to *The Rest*."

Littlejohn found himself describing the club by its abbreviated name like an old member.

He left the other two and cautiously made his way up the bank. It was topped by a hawthorn hedge, now thick with foliage smothered in haws. He chose the thinnest part of one of the bushes and peeped down. He had a full view of the side of the inn and the towpath with its cane chairs and little tables. The setting sun was in his eyes and he waited frowning until he could see clearly.

Here at a height, he really saw what a pleasant place it was. In the distance behind the far bank were country houses and large bungalows and traffic passing along a busy highway. All around was peaceful. The evening sun was shining on the trees and lawns of the houses and in some of

the gardens, games of tennis were going on. The dark green
waters of the canal seemed to flow gently by, although there
was little movement except that made by the little boats
which passed.

The terrace at *The Bargees' Rest* was quiet. There were
about eight people there, sitting in the late sunshine, drinking beer. The sight of it made Littlejohn's throat feel
parched. Myers was there, and Falconer and his wife. Falconer was, as usual, lounging almost full length, his peaked
cap drawn over his eyes. His wife was busy with her embroidery and even as Littlejohn watched, she asked Falconer
to do something and he rose with what seemed lazy reluctance and went inside the club.

Littlejohn found Christine at his elbow. She was smiling.
The first time she'd been really pleasant and human to him
since he'd known her. The promise of a meal had worked
wonders.

"I thought I'd come and see things. I don't think *he* likes
me. . . ."

She pointed in the direction of Father Silvester, who had
settled comfortably under the hedge and was reading his
breviary, lost to the world.

"Is this where Alfie came?"

"Yes. . . . He looked down just like you are."

"Where were you?"

"On the other side of the hedge peepin' through."

"And what did Alfie do or say?"

"There was nobody to say anythin' to. All he did was
give a little whistle to himself."

"As if he was surprised?"

"S'right."

She removed a quid of chewing-gum, stuck it on the
branch of a tree, took four more sticks from her pocket,
screwed them in a mass, and put them in her mouth.

"What do you think he saw?"

"I don't know. . . ."

She said it with difficulty because of the gum which she
was now kneading vigorously between her teeth.

"I could reely do with a smoke. But *he* doesn't like it."

"Did he seem scared of what he saw?"

"Nope. It needed a lot to scare Alfie."

It was like squeezing blood out of a stone!

"What *did* he look like?"

"I dunno. Sort of surprised . . . then pleased. He looked once, then twice again, as though he couldn't believe his eyes. Then he give himself a smile. Like this. . . ."

She made a horrible contortion which conveyed nothing.

"Then, he nodded his head at himself, like this. . . ."

That was a bit better. It indicated, according to the gestures of film gangsters, that someone had better look out.

"Thank you for being so co-operative, Christine."

"You makin' fun of me? Because if. . . ."

"No. I'm grateful."

"An' I'm hungry."

"Let's go, then. . . ."

Falconer was back and was pouring out some beer for his wife. Even as he did it, Littlejohn could see her asking him for something else. It was too far to hear what was said. A jaunty little motor-boat drew in. Mr. Abbott and Miss Browning were sitting in it and Vance was at the controls. He looked ecstatic. Steering his boss and his beloved in one cargo had filled his cup of joy! It was almost like a state procession and only needed fireworks and water-music to greet the royal barge. Even this was not enough to waken Falconer from his stupor. He greeted them in an almost horizontal position.

It was all so pleasant that Littlejohn was reluctant to tear himself away. A couple of little girls passed on the tow-path riding ponies and a young man's elegant cruiser conked out right opposite the terrace below. All he could get it to do was cough and splutter and he grew redder and redder as he tore impatiently at the starter.

"Did you happen to take a look at what was going on at the inn below, Christine, whilst Alfie was up here?"

"I just peeped round the corner down there. It was a bit like it is now."

" Do you recognize anybody you saw that night? "

She looked hard again at the party.

" It's too long since. I think I saw the woman that's down there doin' needlework. She'd got all the wools spread out on the table and was sortin' them out."

" Was the man with her? "

" I don't remember. I thought you said we'd go. . . ."

Back on the road to London again, Littlejohn took the next turn to the right and found they were following a path similar to the one which led to *The Bargees' Rest*. Another sunken road with a rotten asphalt surface, filthy from disuse. At the end, a block of old buildings rose in the air.

" Why it's. . . ."

Christine seemed suddenly to dry-up, as though remembering the last time she'd been there, the ecstasy she'd enjoyed, and the realization that she would never come there with Alfie Batt again.

" Pore Alfie! "

And that was the only expression of grief Alfie ever got from his former girl. She was already thinking of the bliss of bringing Ernie there.

It was Waterbury Wharf.

They all climbed out of the car again.

" Is this the last time? I'm hungry. . . ."

" Come and show me where you and Alfie were hidden."

She dawdled across the head of the wharf and indicated a small plot which might, when the wharf was in its prime, have been the garden worked by some enthusiastic employee. There was still an old-fashioned sprawling white rose-bush there, with a few blooms and a shower of hips scattered across the foliage. The grass beneath had grown long and rank and was sufficient to conceal anyone lying among it. It petered out in sedge, water flags and rushes as it neared what, in wet weather, must have been swampy ground. Now the whole place was parched by the drought.

" We were here. . . ."

She pointed and her eyes strayed round the place.

In the palmy days of the canal it had been a busy little basin, presumably owned or rented by a firm of water-carriers and warehousemen whose old ruined buildings were still standing. There was even a weatherworn sign, nailed to the main warehouse. It was held askew by a single large nail and would soon be down.

> *Crossman and Bicknell*
> *Carriers by Canal to all Parts.*
> *Warehousemen. Barge Hirers.*

You could hardly make out the old painting and several other occupations had worn off the sign.

There was the distinctive smell of canal water over everything. And on top of it the oppressive odour of rust and decay.

The wharf stood on a tributary of the main canal, divided from it by a huge pair of closed sluice gates, rotting, with their metal rusty and their timbers breaking up. A stream of water trickled from the half-closed sluice, and although the levels of the main water and the side-stream seemed the same, it appeared as if the traffic on the larger one continually agitated the smaller. The noise of water was the only sound to disturb the stillness.

The gaunt stone warehouses, all the glass in the windows smashed, stood out stark in the evening light. On the cobbled pavements at the sides of the basin, which had been the dock for barges in days past, heaps of old stone, rubble, and mortar. Grass was growing between the setts. Three tumble-down cranes, the remnants of an old cart, and a large boat, like a lifeboat, submerged and falling to pieces under the water at the dock-head. That was all.

"Where did he throw in the body?"

Christine looked round and pointed.

"I think it was there."

"Did you happen to see it?"

"I said I didn't. He left me lying in the grass. I didn't see anythin'. But I knew where Alfie went."

She had obviously seen more than she would say and was keeping quiet to remain out of trouble.

The spot she had roughly indicated was in one side of the wharf.

The body was found entangled in the broken sluice-gate of Waterbury Wharf.

It was easy to see how it had happened. It had drifted slowly towards the main canal until it met obstruction.

Christine was watching with great interest a pair of lovers pressed in the doorway of an old warehouse, listening, motionless, almost trying not to breathe until the intruders had gone.

" Somebody else knows this place, too. . . ."

Littlejohn didn't seem to hear. This had once been a quiet little world of its own, the tide of commerce had gone out and left it high and dry, useful only now for secret purposes, such as murder and love-making. It was almost like the silent world of the Sleeping Beauty. On the main canal barges and little boats floated past, one of them playing *The Merry Widow* on a gramophone. Lights were beginning to appear in the distant houses. The lovers were still holding their breath. There was nothing here to give a ghost of a clue in the murder witnessed by Alfie Batt.

" Let's go. . . ."

Littlejohn gave it all a last look. Boats had tied-up in the water on the other side of the Waterbury sluice. They were sharply silhouetted in the dusk. Some might have been those of holidaymakers; others more permanent floating summer houses. A woman carried a large bowl of slops and emptied them over the side of a cruiser just moored beyond the sluice, and another was washing and hanging out some clothes on the deck of a work-patrol boat belonging to the canal owners.

Littlejohn wondered if there had been any moored there on the night Plaster was thrown in the wharf.

Next day there was a broadcast request from the B.B.C.

E

Will the owners of any boats moored in or near Water-
bury Wharf, on the Grand Union Canal, on the evening
of May 25th last, between the hours of eight and ten,
kindly communicate with the Metropolitan Police, New
Scotland Yard, or any police station. . . .

It gave rise to extensive crackpot telephoning and hundreds of letters, none of which was any use.

It was almost dark when they started back. The intense
heat of the day had turned to oppressive thundery warmth,
yet it did not rain. The roads were full of cars hurrying
home. Here and there, the customers of wayside pubs had
brought out chairs and were sitting in their shirt-sleeves
with their drinks. Whiffs of beer greeted Littlejohn as he
passed them.

Just before Barnet, Littlejohn pulled-up.

" Christine, is this the road you came back to London on,
on your scooter the night you went to the wharf? "

She had been in a kind of trance, humming a dismal tune,
now and then beating her feet on the floor of the car in a
kind of ecstasy, or twisting her body like the spider lady on
the halls.

" Uh? "

She moved the quid of chewing-gum from one side of her
mouth to the other. In the back seat, Father Silvester was
peacefully asleep. His function seemed to be to keep order.

Littlejohn repeated his question.

Christine looked through the lowered window fixedly, as
though she were thinking hard.

" Yep."

" How do you know? "

" We've driven straight all the way, haven't we? "

" Yes."

" Well. . . ? "

" When you reached Barnet, where did you turn off? "

" I'll show you. . . ."

Littlejohn drove slowly along waiting for the signal.

" Here! "

" How do you know? "

They were at the junction of a side-road and two cafés, their lights now on, stood at the opposite corners of the street. In one of them, a group of teen-agers were drinking what looked like iced drinks.

" I asked Alfie to stop. I wanted my supper. He pretended not to hear."

It sounded quite right. On the map Littlejohn had closely studied before the trip, it was the turning which led to Bastable's house. He followed the road, made a few turns. Christine was humming out of tune again, lost in the arms of an imaginary partner.

He pulled up at the corner of a little square, with young trees planted in holes in the asphalt pavements. Semi-detached houses on three sides, which faced a small park on the fourth.

" Was it here Alfie brought you? "

She looked around again with mock studiousness.

" Nope. This isn't it."

" Why? "

" It wasn't a square. It was a road with houses facin' one another."

" Wait here both of you, if you don't mind."

Littlejohn climbed out of the car and, after a brief search, found the Bastable's house. Selborne, Abbey Crescent. It was a square, not a crescent, but that didn't matter much. A large house, converted into two flats, with a staircase outside leading to the upper one. There was a garden enclosing it. In the front garden, a post with a sign screwed on it. *For Sale.*

On the ground floor a faint light filtered round the drawn curtains. Littlejohn could hear sounds of the news over the radio.

He had obtained the key of the Bastable's flat from the local police earlier in the day. Irma had left it with a request that they should keep an eye on the place. Littlejohn was going to do that just now. He ran up the stairs, let himself in the flat, and switched on the light.

A small hall leading to a long passage, from which four doors led to the rooms. Behind the door, a number of letters; nothing of any importance. Circulars, a coupon for free detergent, and an income-tax demand. A final one, printed in red. Come murder, come death, the wheels of the tax collector continued to turn.

Littlejohn strolled round the place. It smelled airless and not too clean. First, the sitting-room, the furniture of which had been sheeted. A suite, a cocktail cabinet, a wireless set. . . . Littlejohn, his pipe between his teeth, wandered here and there. Nothing. Even the bottles in the cabinet were empty. All that remained were some cocktail cherries in a glass jar. . . .

The small dining-room was the same. A cheap-looking set of chairs and a heavy oak table. A sideboard and bookshelves in one corner. A dismal little place. In the flat below, some-one was moving about and might have been following round the footsteps in the floor above. There was nothing worth noting in the drawers of the sideboard. Littlejohn found himself looking at the books. Banking text-books, old and out of date, book-club novels, seven volumes of an encyclo-paedia. . . . On top of the bookshelves were photographs of Bastable and Irma, both in evening dress, for some reason. Bastable looked like a waiter and Irma like a model posing for an advertisement in a glossy magazine.

Then, the kitchen, very reminiscent of Irma. Not much in the way of home cooking. Tinned goods in the cupboard; everything in readiness for meals without much effort. The small rubbish bin was bulging with refuse. Littlejohn pressed the pedal and quickly released it again. This was whence the stale smell filled the flat. The other two were bedrooms. One for Irma, one for Cyril. Bastable's was the smaller. Littlejohn opened the wardrobe; it was empty. The whole place had, in fact, been cleared. The bed stripped, the drawers cleaned out. The cheap curtains were drawn. The only identification was a safety-razor and a few old blades and some empty patent-medicine bottles on the window-sill. . . .

Littlejohn recoiled momentarily as he opened the next door. A full blast of perfumed toilet articles of all kinds, dominated by Irma's characteristic favourite. This room hadn't been much disturbed. It was like a boudoir. The largest room in the house and overflowing with feminine bric-à-brac. The dressing-table was like the beauty counter in a chemist's shop. Bottles, boxes, scent-sprays, instruments, tubes. . . . And an ash-tray full of rubbish. The wardrobes —there were two—were half empty. Such articles as remained were expensive and bore the labels of high-price makers. But the best had been skimmed off; Irma had taken them to Brighton, or wherever else her fancy had roved. The same with the drawers. Littlejohn felt a bit like a burglar as he casually opened them and turned over the contents. A lot of junk, for the most part. The whole set-up was in poor taste; furnishings, furniture, decorations, pictures. . . . All making the best of small means, expensive ideas badly satisfied by imitations of the real thing. Phoney. . . .

There was a book in the top drawer. Littlejohn thought at first that it was an address book. It turned out to be a suede-backed copy of *The Rubaiyat of Omar Khayyam*. Leaves with gold edges, voluptuous illustrations, a verse a page. . . . The kind of thing fashionable for birthdays before the war. Littlejohn flicked over the pages with his thumb. Some of the verses were marked in pencil. They must have pleased Irma. They dealt with Love and Wine. Those on Death hadn't been touched. One was heavily scored.

> When all the Temple is prepared within,
> Why nods the drowsy Worshipper outside?

And in pencil in the margin, thinly written, *Alec, 6.11.52*. Littlejohn made a note of it on the back of an old envelope.

The bell of the flat rang. Littlejohn closed the door of the bedroom and hastened to answer it.

A small man stood blinking outside on the landing of the staircase. He wore a cap and carried a large stick. By his side, a huge boxer dog. He goggled at Littlejohn, and seemed surprised to find someone so respectable-looking. He'd expected Bill Sikes or someone worse. A woman was standing at the door of the flat below illuminated by the light from the hall.

" Are you all right, Hubert? "

The dog growled and showed his teeth at Littlejohn.

" What are you doing here? "

The man was obviously mustering all the guts he'd got in his efforts to protect his neighbour's property. He gripped his ash-plant tightly and his teeth chattered. The dog watched him closely ready to tear Littlejohn to pieces at a word.

" I'm from the police, sir. We've been asked to keep an eye on the place."

He showed his warrant-card.

The little man's relief was pathetic. He shook hands. The dog began to wag his tail and climbed up Littlejohn and tried to lick his face. He seemed relieved, too.

" Get down, Warrior! "

" You never know, do you? So many desperate characters around these days. Pity about poor Bastable. Sorry for his missus. Nice couple. Good neighbours. . . ."

The man was fighting to recover his breath.

" Like to come down for a drink? "

Littlejohn excused himself, patted the dog, said good-night to Hubert and his wife, and joined Father Silvester and Christine in the car.

" You've been a . . . a long time. I'm dying of hunger."

" You're sure this isn't the place you and Alfie came to? "

" Dead sure. I said so."

" Well, well. We'll have to try another, then."

" I'm hungry. . . ."

Father Silvester leaned over the back of her seat.

" Will you stop whining about your hunger? You can famish for a little longer. I don't wish to hear another word from you about hunger, thirst, or any other of your appetites. . . ."

Littlejohn drove off. Two streets, a long road, a left turn and then. . . .

"Remember this, then, Christine?"

A long suburban stretch, with trees on either side. It was built-up with houses and bungalows of all shapes and sizes. The Superintendent pulled-up at a small detached house with a lawn. There was a scent of roses on the hot air. In front, a street lamp illuminated the wrought-iron gate and drive.

"Of course, I remember it. Alfie passed it on the scooter, then went to the corner there. . . ."

She indicated a side street which turned right from the road.

". . . Then he parked his scooter round the corner and went off quietly into the road again to watch what the bloke did with his car. He was puttin' it in the garage."

"You went with Alfie?"

"Not likely. I wanted to see what Alfie was up to."

"Are you sure?"

"Course I'm sure. I can prove it."

"How can you prove it?"

She uncoiled her body and climbed out.

"Comin'?"

Littlejohn followed her. They went to the side street, down another and found themselves at a corner shop.

"This is it."

"What about it?"

She indicated an advertisement in the window.

Peabody's Potato Crisps

"I told you I was hungry. Still am, by the way. Alfie wouldn't stop, an' I couldn't go on any more. I got some crisps here and a bottle of cissie stuff, non-alcoholic cider. . . . I could find the place in the dark."

"You *have* done, it seems. . . ."

"Have we finished now? When do we eat?"

"Yes, we've finished, Christine, and you've earned your keep. Come on, let's find a place."

She almost ran all the way back to the car.

The house by the lamp was in darkness. Littlejohn walked up the path and rang the bell. There was nobody at home. The noise inside, however, confirmed what he already knew.

Cain and Abel began to snarl and bark in a harsh duet. The house was Falconer's.

11

BANKER'S REPORT

"I'D TRY FESTING, if I were you."

Littlejohn had been enquiring from Mr. Abbott about the set-up at Moorgate six years ago, when Bastable and Myers had been joined there by Falconer, fresh from the north. Abbott had only been chief at Moorgate for four years. The previous manager had been Festing.

"He's now manager of our very large Pall Mall office."

Mr. Abbott wondered whatever had come over the police. Bastable had murdered Plaster and then shot himself out of remorse, either for the killing or for rifling his own till. What did events five years ago matter? It was just beyond Abbott. He was glad to pass the buck to Festing, an acknowledged diplomat. Abbott was vaguely uneasy. For some indefinable reason, he felt himself on the verge of a mighty catastrophe.

The West End branch of the Home Counties Bank was very different from the one in Moorgate. It had been the head office of Pecks', an old and majestic private bank with an aristocratic clientele. Mr. Theodore Festing had succeeded the last decrepit member of the old firm, as manager.

Pecks' premises were almost as they had been a century ago. They were protected by an order for the preservation of ancient monuments, which might have applied to some of their staff as well. Huge mahogany glass-panelled doors with the old Peck crest on them, a hen, rampant, pecking a pile of gold coins.

Graceful Georgian furnishings, large lustre chandeliers, a formidable counter, embellished by brass coin-scales and bright copper shovels, as though, like the wise virgins, Pecks' were keeping their equipment bright for the return of the golden sovereign.

From the walls, the calm and confident faces of dead and gone Pecks in their gilded frames critically examined coming and going clients. The ancient leather fire-buckets stood on the marble floor in the public space to receive waste-paper. Four elderly cashiers in morning dress—two with rosebuds in their coats—were, when Littlejohn entered, attending to a select body of customers. A dignified, elderly attendant in uniform descended upon the Superintendent and, deferential and solemn, led him to the manager.

Mr. Festing was sitting alone in the parlour, once occupied by three partners, whose graceful drum tables now held financial papers and reports. He was a tall, portly man, with a very smooth pink face and a bald head. He, too, wore morning dress and on his chest, like a pectoral cross, dangled a thin monocle on a black cord. He seemed pleased to see Littlejohn and shook him warmly by the hand.

"We depend on you chaps. By gad, we do!" he said. There had been a raid elsewhere the day before.

Abbott had already introduced them over the telephone and explained the purpose of Littlejohn's visit.

"This affair's becoming a thundering nuisance," Mr. Festing had said, but he showed no annoyance to his visitor.

"Sit down and tell me what I can do for you, Superintendent."

It reminded Littlejohn more of Harley Street than Pall Mall. He imagined that Mr. Festing might next gently take his pulse, tell him to put out his tongue, and then order him into a private clinic.

"I believe, sir, you were manager of your Moorgate branch six years ago."

"Yes; Abbott was my assistant, then, and followed me there as manager. A very delightful man."

Festing's voice was very deep and comforting. Quite capable of refusing an overdraft and dismissing a client with a feeling that he had been accorded a favour.

"Do you recollect Bastable, Myers and Falconer, sir?"

" Of course I do. I could have told you then that Bastable and Falconer would end their days on the counter and Myers, made of totally different stuff, would get on. In my day, Myers was bill-clerk; one day he'll be a manager. Mark my words."

"What did you think of Bastable?"

" Poor fellow! I never thought he'd end up by blowing out his brains. . . ."

The bullet had been in the chest, but Littlejohn hadn't the heart to correct Mr. Festing's dramatic cliché.

". . . He was always a defeatist. Afraid of responsibility and, although *de mortuis* etcetera, I always thought he was lazy. No energy. I well remember suggesting that Bastable be given a change and moved to a cashier's post elsewhere to shake him out of his lethargy, but he took it so badly . . . almost had a nervous breakdown . . . that we left him where he was. I suppose he'd started to live above his income. Hence his cash difference."

" Live above his income, sir? "

"Yes. You must know already, he married a flighty and extravagant girl. Big mistake for anyone who wants to get on in a bank, or even remain on the staff, not to have the steadying influence of a good little wife behind him."

Everyone told the same tale. Irma's reputation had travelled far.

"You used the word flighty, sir. . . ."

"All things considered, I think it is the right one. She seemed to have no sense of responsibility. A dangerous flirt and worse. . . ."

Mr. Festing then produced a silver snuff-box, took a pinch, threw half of it away, and sniffed the rest up his handsome nose. Then, he took out a spotless handkerchief of coloured silk and trumpeted in it. It was a refuge of his when he was embarrassed. Snuff, the handkerchief, the trumpets . . . and customers knew the verdict was likely to go against them!

A young lady entered with a tray of tea things and poured them out a cup each.

"Would you care for a biscuit, Superintendent? Don't eat 'em myself. Got to watch my weight. No? Would you prefer a cheroot or a cigar? I smoke cheroots myself. . . ."

A drum of cheroots appeared on the desk as by a feat of prestidigitation. They lit one each and sat back comfortably.

Irma had been left behind. The room was utterly quiet. Deep carpets, double windows, padded doors. The only sound came from the lovely old bracket clock ticking on the Adam mantelpiece.

"And Falconer?"

"Falconer? Ah yes. A man of brains and good taste, I must admit. Cultured, too. Pity he has no ambition. He'd have risen high in the bank, I can assure you. But he didn't *want* to. I can't understand him. Content to remain a cashier."

"Why?"

Mr. Festing puffed his cheroot and carefully deposited a long cylinder of ash in an ancient barber's bleeding-bowl which he used for the purpose.

"Why? I think his marriage was a failure and he lost heart. . . . I'm being very candid with you, Superintendent, and I hope you'll treat all I say as confidential."

"I promise to be discreet, sir."

Discreet! Mr. Festing beamed and was satisfied.

"Falconer came from York and I have friends there who know him well. Good school, good prospects. His father was a wool merchant, who went bankrupt in the slump, and died. Falconer got a job with us. One of our directors at the time was his godfather. Falconer was all set for success. Then he married Fleur Harrison. A lovely girl, but quite unsuitable for him. Spoiled only daughter of a country parson, who'd had six sons before her. He was so delighted with the change that he ruined her. Doted on her. She expected the same treatment from her husband. Required his undivided attention and saw she got it. Nobody else mattered. Falconer was a good musician in those days. Played the guitar. Not a Segovia, of course, but good and promising. He soon gave it up after he married. Fleur said she disliked his strumming.

It's been the same all along. And yet, his treatment of her has been impeccable. A pity. . . ."

"No other women in his life?"

Mr. Festing again resorted to snuff and the turmoil which followed it.

"Is it true there was an affair with Irma Bastable, sir?"

Mr. Festing slipped his monocle in his eye. It made him slightly resemble a carp peeping through a small section of an aquarium.

"He and Fleur lived with the Bastables for a time. Falconer was quite a good-looking chap, in a way, then. He'd poise and a languid kind of charm. When he came to interview me when he was transferred from York branch, he told me Bastable had offered him hospitality till he and his wife could find accommodation. I almost said 'Beware'. Not long after, whilst Fleur was in the north with her people arranging the removal, Falconer and Irma were seen together in the West End. I knew she would set-about him before long. He had the bored imperturbable way which seems to fascinate women."

"It lasted long?"

"No, it didn't. I remonstrated with him. He took it in a calm way which almost put me out of countenance. Said he was merely returning the courtesy of hospitality and giving Irma a meal. Bastable, he said, had toothache and couldn't be there."

The monocle fell from the eye and dangled to rest in its usual place.

"Nothing more was heard of their being out alone together?"

"This sounds like a gossip column, my dear Littlejohn, doesn't it?"

Mr. Festing bared his strong white teeth good humouredly.

"It is important, sir."

"Why?"

"Because I'm investigating a matter which may end in Bastable's being proved a murderer as well as an embezzler and suicide. I wish to know all the background from his friends."

He told the old, old story again. Bastable, Plaster, the teddy-boy, the blackmail.

Mr. Festing thrust his hands out in horror, like someone fending-off evil.

" Surely not! Not Bastable! "

" Why do you say that, sir? "

" Silly, lazy, a hypochondriac. . . . But, not that! Not a murderer! He was too gentle, too well brought-up. His father was a parson. . . ."

Littlejohn almost smiled. The Rev. Hannibal Bastable's eccentric antics were certainly no testimonial for poor Cyril!

" He was always in love with Irma? "

" I believe he was. He must have known she didn't care a hoot about him."

Mr. Festing suddenly grew excited. He slapped his table with both hands and the large ring he wore on one finger sounded like a hammer on the hollow top.

" It's not to be wondered at. He was weakly, timid, complaining. . . . His wife, a passionate, undisciplined—I almost said promiscuous—woman, sophisticated by her life on the stage, ruthless in pursuing her will. Bastable needed someone to mother him. His own mother had a peculiar—I might say rather unhealthy—influence over him. He fell under Irma's spell whilst she was convalescent and presumably lacking in her natural vitality. I know all this, because our Brighton manager was an old friend of mine at the time of Bastable's whirlwind wooing and marriage."

Yet another confirmation of the Bastable story. Mr. Festing was still talking.

" Bastable was always faithful to Irma. I'm sure of it. Right to the end, she was the only woman for him. He was a pitiable complacent cuckold. . . ."

The snuff again appeared to soothe him. He spoke through his handkerchief.

" A cuckold because he was afraid if he exercised his rights as a wronged husband, he would lose her altogether.

That would have been the last stroke of his persistent ill-luck. It would have broken him completely. I would, in spite of all you've told me, say that finally he took his own life because he couldn't bear his love for Irma any longer. You understand me? I'm glad you do. Is there anything more cruel and demoralizing than true-love despised, ungratefully cast back, and shamefully made to seem ridiculous."

Mr. Festing, who was a happily married sentimentalist, gazed mournfully above Littlejohn's head, where hung the portrait in oils of Mr. Sebastian Peck (1784-1815), who had flung himself in the line of fire at Waterloo for love of a disdainful married lady, fifteen years older than himself.

"Did Bastable ever know of Falconer's fancy for Irma?"

"He did. He actually came to me afterwards and tried to explain that Falconer had done no harm. Said he'd merely been kind to Irma during his own indisposition. He'd heard I'd kicked up a row with Falconer and feared I might have him moved from my branch. He pleaded for him. I said in the end, I'd overlook it. But I'm afraid the affair didn't finish at that. It petered out later. I heard many things when it was all over. This is confidential and was confided in me under promise of secrecy. If Fleur had known, I don't know. . . . So you'll er. . . ."

"Be discreet, sir."

"Good. My informant saw Falconer and Irma together actually leaving the home of Irma's mother at Brighton! Whatever they were doing there, I can't think."

He gave Littlejohn a sardonic grin, which belied his statement.

"It's all over now, I suppose, sir?"

"Long ago. There have, I'm sorry to say, been others since. Abbott confided in me. He was greatly distressed and wondered where his duty lay. Should he officially report it, or turn a blind eye? After all, it was not Bastable's misdemeanours; it was his wife's. I advised him not to interfere. Provided, of course, Bastable's work and good name were unsullied. It remained so until the end. And then, his cash was found to be wrong! He must have been off his head with despair. I'm deeply sorry about the whole wretched business."

They both sat silent for a minute. The tragic story of Bastable was almost too sad to bear. Murder, embezzlement, blackmail, suicide. . . . They were all quite out of character with the timid wretched little man, who had once, in his first ecstasy of love, painted Brighton red with a cocotte and then, to her surprise, married her and tried to make her respectable.

" I don't understand it. . . ."

Mr. Festing said it again as he shook hands with Little-john at the door and turned sadly to deal with a duchess who wished to withdraw her famous jewels from safe-custody in the vaults for a party that evening. From a waiting-room emerged a diplomat, followed at a respectful distance by the bank beadle, and carrying curiously shaped tin boxes, also from safe-keeping. They held his cocked hat and sword, for he was attending a levee.

Littlejohn walked slowly back to the Yard. Pall Mall was quiet for the time of day. The sun was still beating down and melting the tar in the roadway. The air was hot and still. It was as if everyone had fled indoors out of the heat and London was in the throes of a siesta until the afternoon brought coolness again. In Trafalgar Square, one solitary sandwichman was parading with his board. *Prepare to Meet Thy God.* And in Whitehall, a guardsman had fainted from the heat and fallen from his horse.

At Scotland Yard, Littlejohn sought out his friend of the Fraud Squad. Superintendent Flight, a name suggesting the end of all frauds.

Flight was in his room scrutinizing a ledger and a lot of invoices. He was without his coat and waistcoat and he had even removed his braces and shoes. He apologized to Little-john.

" If I don't get some relief from the heat very soon, I'll have a stroke. It's bad enough with the weather as it is, but I'm just going through the papers of the Kosy-Heat

Winterwarming Company, the managing director of which has done a bunk to South America with his typist and twenty-five thousand pounds. . . ."

"Ever had anything to do with bank cashiers substantially wrong in their cash, Horace?"

"Dipping their hands in the till?"

Flight was a tall, elderly officer, who had once been an Inspector of Taxes, lost heart, and fled to the force for police protection. He had a long, pale sad face and thin grey hair with a monkish tonsure on the crown. His moustache hung down at each end and he had the expression of a tired spaniel, as though fraud had crushed his spirit. He was carefully dressed in normal weather and always carried a pencil behind his ear.

To illustrate his supplementary question, Flight dipped his long fingers in an imaginary cash-drawer and removed a fistful of invisible banknotes. Then he went on to count them in thin air.

"Yes. And evading discovery in spite of frequent and independent surprise checks."

Flight smiled. It completely altered his appearance, and even made him rather good-looking and debonair.

"Was the cashier in question a conjurer, by any chance?"

"I never heard he was."

"I can't say I've actually encountered any such cases in banks. You see, they keep these things in the family and hush-hush. And they have their own squads of highly expert inspectors to attend to them. As for the accounting side of such crimes, even there, the banks are very reluctant to expose their books to outsiders. I've even known them drop cases rather than betray the secrets of their clients to independent accountants."

"Yet, the culprit in the case I'm investigating, reputed to be a slow-witted man, evaded them for quite a time."

Flight nodded cheerfully, like an expert who admires the tricks of a good animal in the ring at a dog show.

"Clever! I've come across one or two cases in merchant banks who've called us in, and then, of course, I've quite a number of friends who're bank inspectors. Matter of fact, one sings next to me at our glee-club."

"Has he confided in between the madrigals?"

"When I sing, I forget this place. No; I'll look-up some cases for you and let you know. We'll have a chat tomorrow over a glass of beer. You can pay for it."

"Can't you remember a single case off-hand? This affair keeps being put-off and put-off."

"I did know a man who borrowed the money elsewhere and put back his defalcation a day or two before his inspectors checked his till. Then he repaid it when it was over and borrowed it again next month. He guessed right three times; the fourth he was two days late. He got two years. Any good?"

"Might have been if the borrowing was for a hundred or so; but this involved a thousand pounds."

"Chicken-feed compared with Kosy-Heat. I do remember another case, too, come to think of it. This fellow, a teller in a private bank in the city, was two thousand wrong in his cash. He put it right by forging a cheque on a dormant account for two thousand. The dormant account was chosen because it was unlikely that the passbook or pass-sheet would be asked for by the customer and the fraudulent withdrawal discovered. You follow, don't you? Such a transaction was as if the cashier had drawn the cash from the dormant account and put it in his till to make up the difference. Unfortunately for him, a week after he'd pulled the trick, the passbook was asked for. I think he got five years. You see, forgery was involved, and the courts always treat forgers sternly. . . ."

"May I use your 'phone, Horace?"

"Of course."

Littlejohn asked for the Home Counties, Moorgate; Mr. Abbott. When the manager answered, he told him the trick revealed by Flight.

"I'm sorry, Superintendent, but when I was a junior clerk, a colleague of mine, aged twenty-one and doing relief duty on a till, used such a device to obtain five hundred pounds.

His father paid-up and he thus avoided prosecution. I ought to add, his father was a wealthy customer, took his son in his own business, and he is now, I understand, a millionaire. So, it's an old dodge, you see. We checked all the accounts for such entries after poor Bastable's shortage came to light. Nothing. Myers, by the way, told me of your meeting last night and that you'd asked him to look out for any strange entries in the books. We're just engaged in going through them again. I'll let you know. . . ."

Littlejohn turned to Flight.

" Your scheme's a chestnut, Horace."

" As I said, I'm not used to bank frauds, because they deal with them in secret. But I'm going to the glee-club tonight. We've just begun rehearsing *Phaudrig Crohoore* and I'll tackle Hooley when we pause for breath. Hooley's the bank inspector, by the way. I'll be after you in the morning with the news."

" If you survive *Phaudrig Crohoore*. How does it go. . . ? "

> Phaudrig Crohoore was the broth of a boy,
> And he stood six feet eight.
> His arm was as round as another man's thigh,
> 'Tis Phaudrig was great. . . ."

A wild light came in Flight's eyes.

" How do *you* know it? It's most unusual and we thought it would be a musical surprise for everybody. Did you . . . ? "

" Yes. I used to be in the Metropolitan Police Choir myself. . . ."

And Littlejohn left Flight to recover.

12

THE COAL-HOLE IN TIPE'S ALLEY

THE AFTERNOON WAS worse than the morning. It was
stifling and there wasn't a breath of air. The streets and the
river shimmered in the sunshine and passers-by staggered
along exhausted. London was in the throes of holidays.
Cromwell had gone to Cornwall that morning. All the windows of Scotland Yard were open, except those of Chief
Superintendent Naysmith, who was always cold and complaining of draughts in any kind of weather.

Littlejohn was in his shirt-sleeves torpidly browsing over
a report. He added his signature and put back his pen in
his pocket. Then, the telephone rang.

It was Falconer.

" I badly want to see you, Superintendent. About the
whisky bottle which vanished the other night. . . ."

" You took it? "

" Yes; but I can't explain now. The 'phone's in the main
office. Could we meet later? "

Since Christine had identified Falconer's house, and not
Bastable's, as the scene of Alfie Batt's intrigue, Littlejohn had
been anxious to call on Falconer there. But he couldn't find
an excuse. If he'd asked for a rendezvous and another talk,
Falconer would, ten-to-one, have suggested *The Bargees'
Rest*.

" Shall I call on you at home tonight? It's a bit awkward
talking things over at the *Rest*, isn't it? If you'll tell me
where in Barnet your place is, I don't mind coming out at
all. It'll be a change."

Falconer hesitated. Littlejohn was sure he was wondering
how his wife would take it.

" Will you really? We'll be jolly glad to see you. Or to save you the trouble, I could join you at the Yard, and we could dine together in town."

"I'm afraid I'm pulled out of the place just now. Holidays here as well as elsewhere. Besides, London's like an oven. . . ."

"That's right. Shall I pick you up there?"

"No; don't wait. I'll come out by car at a little after eight."

What to do meanwhile. Littlejohn looked at his watch. Four o'clock. He had plenty of work. Odd cases to clear-up, reports to finish. And yet, the Bastable affair was becoming a bore and an obsession, which wouldn't leave his mind.

A thousand pounds! What had Bastable done with it? There wasn't a trace of it. Had Irma had it? Or Plaster? Or some other unknown to whom Bastable owed money? Among the effects found on the body after Bastable's suicide, there had been a note-case and a small pocket diary. The rest of the inventory was in Littlejohn's drawer in a memorandum. Nothing. The usual contents of a man's pockets. The note-case had contained three one-pound notes, a season ticket on the train, a visiting-card or two, and a driving-licence. No wallet at all, and Irma had confirmed that Bastable had not carried one for years. The little diary revealed nothing. Telephone numbers of a harmless kind, pathetic calculations as to how Bastable was going to spend his salary every month, and no lead from the figures. Memoranda of appointments, all completely humdrum and pointless. The whole of the contents of the dead man's pockets lacked any interest at all. They revealed him as living a dreary existence with not a single purple patch or red-letter day in it. No interest or hope in life.

And yet, a thousand pounds! Where had it gone?

The case itself had not been investigated on lines which, at Scotland Yard, were almost a ritual. Littlejohn had painted-in the background of Bastable's forlorn and despairing existence.

Irma and her affairs; the daily round at the bank; the early days and career of the dead man; his home and family life, if such it could be called; his association with the dramatic society and *The Bargees' Rest*.

Nothing unusual had come to light. A blank. . . . Except the thousand pounds, and now the astonishing fact that Alfie Batt had fetched-up at Falconer's house instead of Bastable's on the night the blackmail began. Could Bastable have called on Falconer on the evening he threw Plaster's body in the canal?

Littlejohn picked-up the telephone and asked for Mrs. Utting's number at Brighton. Irma's mother answered.

" How are you, Superintendent? Do you want me, or is it Irma, because she's out."

" Could I get hold of her by any chance? "

" She's gone to Mr. Peppercorn's office. I think there's somebody biting at the house at Barnet. I do hope she sells it. It upsets her every time she goes down there. You wouldn't believe. . . ."

The sympathetic warm voice, which almost enveloped you like a mother's arms!

" Do you know Peppercorn's number, Mrs. Utting? "

She gave it to him and he bade her good-bye and put through another call.

" Is Mrs. Bastable there? "

She was. She even had an attractive telephone manner. The same husky, pleasant voice, as ever.

" May 25th? That's rather a tall order, Superintendent. I really don't know where I was that night."

" Don't you keep a diary, Mrs. Bastable? "

" Yes, of course, but. . . . Wait a minute. I'll get my bag."

He could hear her speaking to someone else in the background. Probably Peppercorn. Then she was back.

" May 25th. . . . Yes. I came down to Brighton to see mother."

And probably the ubiquitous Peppercorn, as well!

" Did you go by road? "

" I always do. I remember, I didn't get a lift that day and I took our own car. Why? "

Littlejohn ignored the question.

"Did you stay the night?"

He needn't have asked it! Probably Peppercorn could have answered that if he'd cared to be truthful.

"Yes. Mother gets lonely, you know."

Of course, she does! Littlejohn, doodling on his scribbling-pad, drew an unctuous curving Irma and put a little ellipse over her head like a halo.

"Did your husband sleep in the flat alone?"

"Wherever is all this leading, Superintendent?"

"I'll tell you when I see you."

He put two graceful arms on his little caricature, held out to receive him.

"Well, Cyril stayed with the Falconers. Alec always said he was welcome to their spare bed whenever he needed it. Cyril had told him I'd be away for the night, so. . . ."

"Thank you very much, Mrs. Bastable."

"Are you sure you won't tell me what it's all about?"

"Not over the telephone. . . . *Au revoir.* . . ."

He finished the sketch by crossing out one arm and adding another, this time waving a tender farewell.

He lit his pipe, took out his notes on the case, and sat back and carefully read them again.

At *The Bargees' Rest* and at the Moorgate Branch of the bank, he'd seen most of the principals of the Bastable drama. And then he came across a name, easily neglected because it appeared only once.

Mrs. Casabon, the cleaner, who'd found the body.

He picked up the telephone again. Mr. Abbott this time. Yes, he could give him the address. One minute.

"Here we are. 12, Knight's Buildings, Friday Street, Kennington. I believe it's just near the Oval. Why, has something else turned-up?"

Littlejohn evaded the question and bade Mr. Abbott a rather hasty good-bye. Then he rang down for a car.

Friday Street was a seedy one and it was even hotter there. Like an oven. Swarms of children on holidays playing in the roadway, women standing at doorways seeking a breath of cool air in vain and talking about the heat. The smells of a vast hive of humanity, overlaid by the fumes of frying bacon emerging from one of the houses.

Number 12 was a tenement in a large block. A drab sort of building, four storeys high, with a modern laundry on the ground floor in which women were sitting gossiping or reading magazines whilst washing-machines churned their dirty linen.

Mrs. Casabon lived on the second floor and, as Littlejohn climbed the wide stone staircase with its brown tiled walls, heads came out from doorways here and there, women with little to do but keep a check on comings and goings and compare notes among themselves about their neighbours' visitors. Children of all ages and sizes ran up and down the steps.

Littlejohn tapped on the door, which opened to reveal a small, clean woman, with a lined pale face and a tired smile. She glanced anxiously at her visitor, thinking of corporation officials, rent collectors, interfering seekers after social information, welfare officers. . . .

" May I have a word with you, Mrs. Casabon? It's about the bank."

She looked more put-out than ever. She wondered if her job was in jeopardy.

" Come in. . . ."

She was wearing an apron and wiped a chair with it.

" Sit down, sir."

A small room serving as living-room and behind it, what seemed to be a scullery. A number of pieces of shabby furniture here and there and a sewing-machine in one corner. A wireless set was talking. An author grumbling about his troubles and how difficult it was to make ends meet these days. Mrs. Casabon wasn't taking much notice. The mere noise seemed to comfort her. The window was open admitting the hullabaloo from the street.

" Could you tell me in your own words, Mrs. Casabon, what happened the night you found Mr. Bastable's body in the cellar of the bank? "

She looked relieved. If it was simply down-to-earth information he wanted and not a lot of nonsense about how much she earned, how she spent her spare time, what political party she favoured, or whether or not she liked the idea of more nationalization, she felt all right. She paid her way, she had four children all married and far away, she rarely saw them, and she went to the catholic church regularly. She was prepared to tell Littlejohn all that by way of introduction to her character and means, but the printed lists which some enquiring busybodies filled-in carefully and carried away, made her tremble with fear. All she wanted was to be left alone.

"I found Mr. Bastable dead, poor gentleman. He was always decent to me and never forgot me at Christmas, which can't be said for all of them."

"What time would that be?"

"I told the police when they was fillin'-in the coroner's remarks. Six o'clock. I heard St. Michael's-in-Cornhill strikin' the hour."

"There was nobody else there?"

"No, sir. His poor body was all alone in that great buildin', with not so much as a soul to say a prayer for him."

"You sent for the police right away?"

"I did. There he was, lying face up, holding a pistol with both hands to his breast. I knew he was dead and I didn't stop. I telephoned 999. I've been through all this before and I know what to do."

She cast her eyes on an enlarged photograph of her late husband, looking astonished, which hung over the fireplace. The drooping moustaches, the fagged air, the frightened eyes of the late Casabon gave him the appearance of having all the cares of the world on his shoulders.

"He was a porter in Billingsgate, sir," she said, seeing that Littlejohn's glance had followed her own.

"He got a knock on the head with a fish-box, sir. It drove him queer. Hung himself. . . ."

She said it in a dreary monotone which made him sorry for her and the state in which she had been left.

"We 'ave to do the best we can. I'm very comfortable at the bank and they're very good to me."

She must have been turned sixty and, at one time, she had doubtless, in her own way, been pretty. Care and age had added a mask of weariness and failing health.

"There was nothin' I could do. They took away the body after making a lot of measurements and examinations. I waited, because suicide or no suicide, the bank 'as to be clean for when they open next day. I waited and got on with me work when it was all over. I was there till past ten. Mr. Abbott, that's the manager, paid me overtime for it. He's a very nice gentleman, sir."

"Did you notice anything peculiar about the place that night, Mrs. Casabon?"

"I can't say I did, sir. If there had been, I wouldn't have seen it, like as not. All those police, people, doctors, coroners, and some of the men from the bank as arrived, too, sort of confused me. And me with me work to do after it all."

"You found the body . . . ?"

"Yes. Face upwards, blood on his poor hands and clothes, stone dead."

"Nothing else?"

"I don't know what you mean, sir."

"Nothing lying there beside it?"

"No, sir. Should there be?"

"Not particularly. The strongroom doors were closed and locked?"

"They were closed, sir. And when the police came, I saw one of the constables try the doors and find them fast. Mr. Bastable's keys was in his pocket and after Mr. Falconer got there. . . ."

"What time would that be?"

"After eight, sir. You see, they wanted his key to open the doors. They use two keys. Mr. Bastable had one and Mr. Falconer the other. Mr. Falconer was at home when they telephoned him and he came right away."

"The staff go out by the side door?"

"Yes."

"And you have a key and enter by it when you arrive to do your work, Mrs. Casabon."

"That's right."

"I've forgotten where the side door is."

"It's in Moorgate, too, sir. Next door to the big main bank doors. There's no side street. The bank's part of a block."

"So, everybody coming and going has to use the Moorgate doors?"

"That's right."

"Nobody could get in or out unseen by anyone watching in Moorgate?"

He thought of Alfie Batt, on his vigil on the night Bastable died.

"Nobody could get in or out, except. . . ."

"Except?"

Mrs. Casabon gave him a tired smile.

"I was thinkin' of Mr. Lett. He was a cashier. Proper caution and he turned to drink. Drunk in the middle of the day, he was, in the end. And him afraid to come in by the front door in case Mr. Festing, who was then the manager, and a very nice gentleman, too . . . in case he should see him and sack him on the spot. I've been at the Moorgate bank twenty years, sir, and I've heard them talk about the old staffs. Some of them was lively lads, sir. None like 'em now."

"What happened to Mr. Lett?"

"Oh yes, Mr. Lett. Some of the others did their best for him. They used to look out for him comin' in from his lunch, which was totally liquid, sir, judging from his condition. Then they'd lead him round the alley. You see, both doors bein' in Moorgate, Mr. Festing might see him comin' in that way. At the back, in Tipe's Alley, there's a coal-hole. His friends used to push Mr. Lett down it, some inside caught him, dusted him down, and then put him in the clerk's room to sleep it off. It couldn't go on for long, though, could it, sir? One day, Mr. Festing happened to come down to the strongroom just as poor Mr. Lett was appearin', feet-first, down the coal-hole. That finished him. He got the sack and he didn't last long after it. He was a gentleman, Mr. Lett was. Always called me by my first name. 'Well, Clotilda,' he'd say in his merry way. I was sorry when I heard he was dead, and I remembered him in my prayers. . . ."

" Is the coal-hole still there? "

" It's there, but there's never any coal comes down it now. I don't know why it wasn't done away with when the place was re-built, but somebody said it was useful in case of fire for the hoses to be put down. So it was left as it was. They put in oil-furnaces for the heating when they modernized the bank. It made a lot less work for me without all that dust and dirt. And the police, on the night Mr. Bastable did away with himself, must have examined it, too. They left it open. . . ."

" Left it open? "

" Yes. You fasten it down on the inside by hookin' a chain through a loop in the lid. The chain was loose when I come to see to things next mornin'. I always look at that chain, sir. It was a habit of mine when we used coal. I was last in at night and I always thought that hole, if left loose, would be a good place for robbers to get in. I still look at it every night."

" The night before, when you examined it, was the chain fixed? "

" I don't remember. But I'm sure I looked at it and if it had been loose, I'd have noticed and fastened it."

" How did you fasten it usually? "

" It's never been loose for years. Not since we got oil and stopped usin' it. In the old days, it was simple. You took the steps . . . or rather *I* did, and climbed up the slope on them to the trapdoor. The slope is a kind of chute the coal came down in those days and then it was shovelled in the furnace room. The men, of course, when they handled Mr. Lett, being more nimble than me, could climb up the slope without a ladder, some of them, although it was dusty. . . ."

" Well, that's most useful, Mrs. Casabon, and I'm grateful for your help."

He gave her a couple of pound notes which she tried to thrust back on him.

" I don't want pay for helpin' the bank, sir. Though I don't see much help I've been. . . ."

He put the money back in the pocket of her apron, shook hands, and bade her good-bye.

On the way down, a crowd of children followed him, eager to be of any service to him, touting for something to do to earn an odd shilling.

At the front door a man was selling winkles.

" Fresh from the sea. . . ."

He drove back into the city and parked his car, after hunting here and there frantically to find a place, in a space left by a pantechnicon which had been moving filing-cabinets.

Tipe's Alley ran parallel with Moorgate, behind the bank. A narrow, squalid thoroughfare, housing shabby warehouses and with all kinds of strange trades being carried-on in little shops and cellars. It took Littlejohn some time to take his bearings and fix in the alley the exact spot behind the Moorgate frontage of the bank. He found it at length.

By some queer leasehold freak, there was a dark, ancient saddler's shop on the ground floor, street level, directly behind the Home Counties. Littlejohn stuck his head in at the door and, peering in the gloom, could make out an old man with a bald head, wearing an apron and steel-framed spectacles, busy at work on a sheet of leather. The aromatic smell of good material pervaded the shop.

" Is the Home Counties Bank between you and Moorgate? "

" Yes. Why? "

" I'm interested in the history of this quarter."

" You've got a job on. Goes back to the Romans, and this shop made saddles for Cromwell's horsemen when London was on the Parliament side."

" Under here. . . . What's there? "

" The bank cellars. Money down there, if you know how to get at it. But it's feet thick in reinforced concrete. I had to find temporary premises when they re-built the bank. Paid me well, but it was awkward for customers. They wanted to buy me out and take the shop, but I refused. My family's been here for three hundred years. Oh, you might think I haven't any business nowadays. But let me tell you, I've all the work I can manage to turn me hands to. . . ."

" The manhole on the pavement leads down to the bank? "

" Old coal-hole. They forgot to make it up when they re-built."

" Never used now? "

" Not for years. Though when I came to work one morning this spring it looked as if somebody had been trying if it would open. There'd been a lot going on there in the night. Cashier shot himself. You'd perhaps see it in the papers."

" Yes. How did you see someone had been opening it? "

" Well, you'll observe now the nick between the trapdoor and the edge of the hole, is full-up with dirt. Every time the pavements are swept, there's dirt and dust piles up there. That morning, I noticed the dirt had been disturbed. In fact, it had got hard, you see, and some of the dirt was so compressed with being there so long, that it had got solid and had come out in the shape of part of a circle. It broke as the trap was raised, but you could see the shape of the round hole, like. . . ."

He picked-up a pair of stirrups and carefully fitted them in the leather he had been preparing.

13

NOTHING IN COMMON

MRS. FALCONER OPENED the door. She looked as lovely and fresh as ever and was wearing a becoming white, flowered frock. She seemed surprised to see Littlejohn.

"Do you wish to speak to my husband?"

So Falconer hadn't told her of his visit!

A small square hall with a staircase rising from one side and, behind, the kitchen. Two doors leading to the dining-room and the lounge. There seemed to be a clash of tastes in every room. A few good pictures on the walls and choice pieces of furniture here and there, and the rest a con-glomeration of commonplace knick-knacks from all over the world. Brassware, native weapons, figures by mediocre or even primitive potters, and odds and ends of glass and china which might have been bought from a chain store or a cheap souvenir shop. Somebody must have been collect-ing junk all over the earth! Mature taste swamped by the infantile.

"Superintendent Littlejohn wants to see you, Alec."

She spoke into the lounge, pushed Littlejohn before her, and followed him in.

This room was the same as the hall. A confusion of tastes in furniture, pictures and ornaments. The embroidered cover was lying on an empty chair where, presumably, Mrs. Falconer had left it when she went to answer the door. Two standard lamps with shades made from old parchment legal documents. Incongruous on the walls, a couple of repro-ductions of Toulouse-Lautrec pictures; one of *Moulin de la Galette*; the other, *A La Mie*, with a lounging couple so dissolute as to be burlesque.

159

" I don't know why he insists on keeping those horrors on the wall. One day I'll burn them."

Fleur had seen Littlejohn eyeing the pictures. His own Toulouse-Lautrec, a racecourse scene, would have been much more presentable in a room like this than those fancied by Alec. *A La Mie* might have been a caricature of a more depraved Alec and Fleur if things went wrong. Boredom, despair, dejection and the bottle. A lot more souvenirs all over the shop. Engraved stools from Ashanti, boomerangs from Australia, a tiger-skin hearthrug, and a small stuffed crocodile hanging from a nail beside the fireplace. Someone had been on safari with a vengeance.

Falconer had been sitting on the other side of the fire-place from his wife, reading a soft-backed, well-soiled book, obviously French, and probably his eternal Proust. He was smoking a cigarette. Over the arm of his chair was clipped a wretched little ash-tray affair to prevent his dropping ash on the carpet. He rose quickly and held out his hand to Littlejohn.

" Hullo, Superintendent. Good of you to call. . . ."

Then, he turned to Fleur.

" He said he might call."

His tone was apologetic and she made no answer. Some-how, when his wife was around, Falconer was more subdued; just as nonchalant as ever, but careful what he said and did. He looked out of place in his surroundings. A room with three different patterns of paper on the walls and ceiling, and a green carpet which clashed with the rest of the decorations.

His wife smiled pleasantly at Littlejohn.

" Hasn't it been a nice day again? How long is this weather going to last? Have you had your holidays yet . . . ? "

Formal and banal.

There was no suggestion of offering drinks. Falconer looked at his wife and then at Littlejohn who, at her invitation, was now sitting in a chair like a tub, his huge body threatening to burst the thing asunder at any moment.

"It's a bit hot indoors. What do you say if we go out for a drink, Superintendent?"

Falconer smiled invitingly at Littlejohn and then glanced at his wife. She shrugged her shoulders and looked at the Superintendent as if to say,

"You see how he is. Always on the bottle. . . ."

"Yes, if you like."

Falconer looked relieved.

"There's a pub just round the corner where they keep good beer. It'll be nice and cool on a night like this."

Outside, cars kept whizzing past and now and then, a large red bus rambled by and shook the whole house. In the room behind, the poodles started to bark. They had evidently been thrust there when Littlejohn rang. Now they were starting to fight again.

"Go and let out Cain and Abel, Alec. Let them have a run in the back garden. . . ."

Falconer rose and went off without a word. Fleur smiled at Littlejohn again.

"Don't let him drink too much. He gets worse and worse. I've told him I won't have it in the house, now. It no sooner arrives, than the bottle's empty."

Falconer was back. He glanced from his wife to Littlejohn, questioning if they had been talking about him. Then, he smiled. It was like the smile of a clown at the circus trying to please the children in the audience.

He kissed his wife. A peck on the cheek. She avoided anything else.

"I won't be long away."

There was a large hotel at the end of the road.

"Sorry to have to take you out. My wife doesn't like our having much in the house. She's been brought up a bit strait-laced you know. Her father was very strict with them."

The landlord of the pub greeted Falconer like an old friend and so did a number of the regulars in the mixed crowd which milled around three deep at the bar. It was evident that Falconer was a frequent attender.

F

"Same as usual. . . . And you, Superintendent."

"Same for me."

They found a little table by the window and sat there with their drinks. Bottled beers, deliciously cool.

Falconer's elbows were on the table. He watched Little-john sipping his beer, as though urging him to get a move on and have a few more.

"I'm sorry to drag you out here, Superintendent, but I had to see you and it wasn't convenient to say what I have to say over the telephone or in the office. You see, it was I who took the bottle of whisky from Bastable's locker."

The tone was steady and bored as usual. He sounded as if he'd made a simple mistake and expected to be excused now that he'd mentioned it.

"Why?"

"You see, we always helped one another out when our personal stocks of whisky and the rest ran out. It's quite a stretch to the nearest place for further supplies. On Satur-day, I found my whisky was low and I remembered Bastable had a half-filled bottle in his locker when he was last at the *Rest*. I didn't want to borrow any elsewhere, because we'd so many people there, it hardly seemed fair to trespass on others. My key fitted Bastable's locker. He was always forgetting his and borrowing mine. Myers told me about your wanting to take the bottle and finding it missing. I'm sorry. I emptied it, and threw it in the dust-bin as we left."

"That's all right. I don't suppose it would have yielded anything useful. But the reason I suggested I might come out here to see you was that I want to ask you a question or two which might assist us. You know our present problem?"

Falconer drank off his beer.

"I'll just get two more. Won't be a minute."

He gangled to the bar, gently and without any effort moved aside the crowd, and was soon back with the drinks. He gave Littlejohn a frank and friendly smile.

"Good health! You were saying about developments. Yes;

the story of Bastable's throwing Plaster's body in the wharf has leaked out. It astounded us all. . . ."

He didn't look astounded. On the contrary, he was calm and collected, gently pouring out the beer.

"Plaster's body was thrown in the canal on May 25th. That's the date the teddy-boy saw it done. You've heard about the teddy-boy?"

"Yes."

"Bastable was staying at your place overnight on that date, wasn't he?"

"Yes. I'm dead sure of that because, I must confess, I've looked it up. You see, I'm a bit interested in crime myself. My godfather was Chief Constable of the county. Not much reason for my interest, but it'll do. When I knew the date, I looked up what I was doing myself. I stayed-in all night; that is, with the exception of my usual call here for half-an-hour for a nightcap. You see, Bastable had borrowed my car. Irma had gone to Brighton in his; that's why we offered him a bed. We were sorry for him, the way she left him on his own with a tin of sardines for his evening meal, so we invited him. About eight, or a little before, he asked if he might use my car. He'd an errand Irma had asked him to do. He didn't say what it was. Well. . . . My car's not worth much. I let him take it. He got back about ten."

"Did he seem disturbed, at all?"

"No more than usual."

"I see. Now may I ask you something very personal? I've had to investigate every aspect of this case, in view of the Plaster angle. Shortly after you came south with your wife, you stayed for a time with the Bastables. Did you have an affair with Irma whilst you were there?"

Falconer's face expressed neither embarrassment nor surprise.

"Shortly afterwards. Yes. . . ."

He gave Littlejohn a whimsical look.

"I was hardly cad enough to carry-on with her under Bastable's own roof. It was afterwards. She was good fun and we got on well together. Before I knew where we were,

I was taking her out. The first time, it's rather an exciting adventure; then, somehow, you're in it up to the neck. Especially with Irma. It took me quite a while to shake myself free. Luckily, there was someone in the offing more fascinating than I was. *She* broke it off, in a tender little speech. Said she didn't want to ruin my life and talked about Fleur and how much she liked her."

" But she *had* ruined it. . . ."

For the first time, Falconer couldn't find anything to say. He had the same *Pagliacci* look, but now it was full of hopeless despair. Bimbo in a quandary!

"Yes."

"Your wife found out."

"Yes. She talked of going home and of divorce. But she had no money. Nor had I. My pay barely keeps us going. I guess my tastes are above it. Anyhow, I put it to her that a divorce would get me the sack from the bank, and that if she left me, it would get round and ruin my chances. Besides, I hadn't the money to keep two homes going. She finally agreed to overlook it. . . ."

" On her terms? "

Falconer gave Littlejohn a grateful look. It was easy to talk to the Superintendent. Falconer didn't even ask how he knew. He took it for granted.

" We've never been suited. She's a decent girl, well brought-up, but her home was a severe and stuffy one and the atmosphere soaked right into her. I guess I'm what you'd call a man of the world. She just doesn't understand breadth of mind, which, I suppose, decent people call licence . . . or that's what my sort of breadth of mind amounts to. Anyhow, she's made me toe the line and do as she wishes. Even now, when I take too much, and it isn't often, she threatens to leave me and get a divorce. . . . I've not much longer to go before I draw my pension. We've got to hang on till then. After that, if she can't put-up with me any longer, she can do as she likes."

It explained everything. Falconer's patient attentions to Fleur; her weary endurance of him; her lack of interest in all he did. And it accounted for Falconer's lackadaisical ways, his philosophical and bored acceptance of life, his heavy drinking to forget his plight.

" . . . I was in an exciting job in the war. I was a liaison officer with the French Underground. I was dropped there five times and brought back. It was hard to settle down when it was all over."

" Where was your affair with Irma carried-on? "

Falconer smiled as though, looking back, he saw something which tickled his sense of humour in it all.

" At Brighton. Her mother had an operation and was away about six weeks. Fleur was in the north at the time, nursing her mother. Irma suggested to me that she returned our hospitality. My God! She returned it to some tune. With interest ! ! "

" Did Bastable get to know? "

" Not the whole of it. But he guessed. The sure sign that he knew about any of Irma's affairs was that he started to whine about making ends meet, asked for a small loan, and then came again when that had gone. It was blackmail, you know, but Bastable hadn't the nerve to play it hard. Ten pounds now and then was the extent of his borrowing. And when the affair petered out, so did Bastable's whining to me. He transferred his lamentations elsewhere. But the funny thing was, he never seemed mad with me. For years, he and I worked side by side as tellers. And yet he was always friendly and polite. He almost went out of his way to be matey. He was so potty about Irma that he was afraid that if he kicked-up a row, she'd go for ever. He couldn't have stood it."

" Was that why he killed himself? "

" No. I don't think so. . . ."

" *Did* he kill himself? "

Falconer looked surprised, but there was no excitement in it. Just a kind of pained glance as though Littlejohn were trying to pull his leg.

" What do you mean? You know as much about that as I do."

"No, I don't. You were the last to see him alive. What did he say as you left him?"

"Nothing out of the ordinary. It was so ordinary, that I can't even remember it."

"You're not telling me the truth, Falconer. Suppose you tell me what actually happened."

Falconer gave him a reproachful stare, like somebody whose pal had just called him a liar.

"I've told it all before to the police and the coroner."

"Very well, I'll have to tell *you*. Didn't Bastable come whining to you again that night you were both putting away the cash . . . alone in the bank?"

"I don't remember. Life was one long whine with Cyril. . . ."

"He was wrong in his cash, remember. He was short of money. His wife was having yet another affair with a chap called Peppercorn. Did he try to borrow from you?"

"He might have said he was hard-up. I was busy putting away the cash."

He was off for two more beers and this time he wasn't looking as confident. He had a fixed expression on his face like a somnambulist.

"Here we are. I'm sorry. I'm not being very helpful, but it's quite a time since it all occurred."

"Not so long that you can't remember the drama played-out in the bank basement that night. Bastable had been begging or whining to you. He was a hysterical man, a neurotic. He liked putting on an act. He took the old revolver from the strongroom and loaded it. Then he threatened to shoot himself. He hoped you'd cave-in and do something for him. Instead, you tried to take the gun from him and it went off. A man like Bastable, play-acting with the gun, would never have pointed it to his heart, nor, had he been serious, would he have done it that way. He'd have threatened to blow his brains out. And, he wouldn't have clutched the gun with both hands like a vice. He gripped it that way because someone was trying to take it from him, and that's why he was shot in the heart, too. You were the only one there. Was it an accident, or did you do it deliberately?"

Falconer was still unshaken. He seemed to be pondering something. Then,

"It was as you say. He tried to borrow from me. I told him I hadn't got a bean. He began the old tale. How I'd alienated Irma's love, how much it cost him to keep her going, how there was another fellow pestering her, Peppercorn. He said he wanted to take her on the Continent for a swell holiday, a second honeymoon and make her forget Peppercorn. As if that would work. I told him so. I told him to punch Peppercorn on the nose. He worked himself up, and finally rushed in the safe, brought out the gun, and pointed it to his head. I thought it wasn't loaded, but couldn't risk it. I knew it was defective and made a grab at it. He fought like a tiger and . . . well . . . the thing went off."

"Why didn't you tell that to the police?"

"What a hope! It would have come out about my earlier affair with Irma. I was sure of that. In any case, I'd have got the sack and I haven't got a bean."

"So, you scrambled through the coal-hole and cleared off through the maze of alleys behind Moorgate?"

"You've found out that, too! I've got to hand it to you, Superintendent!"

Falconer gave Littlejohn an almost jolly, admiring look, as though he'd just heard of a smart trick from an old friend.

"Why go that way?"

"I wanted to avoid the awkwardness of being the last man there. If I'd scuttered out by the Moorgate door, I'd have been seen. I'd very little time. I just locked-up the strongroom with Bastable's and my own keys, put Bastable's back in his pocket, and made off. Mrs. Casabon was due any minute. It was a near shave."

He was thoroughly bored and disgusted. He'd made no fight to hold-up his end, told no more lies to conceal what he'd done. He'd simply thrown-up the sponge in despair.

"And that's all there was to it. I'm sorry I held-out on

the police. Bastable did shoot himself. I hope you'll take my word for it. He was clutching the damned gun so hard that he pulled the trigger. I couldn't believe it at first. . . ."

"I ought to arrest you, Falconer, for perjury in the coroner's court, to begin with. . . ."

"I can only say I'm sorry about it. It seemed to me, at the time, the best way of keeping out of trouble and fuss."

Which was true to character. All Falconer had asked for since his wife had found him out, was to be left in peace, to idle and drink, and lounge about and let the world and its troubles pass him by.

"There's one more thing. . . ."

Falconer cocked his head and waited patiently.

"Did you owe Plaster money?"

Falconer shrugged his shoulders.

"How much more do you know? Yes, I owed him seven hundred pounds."

"How did you manage to do that?"

"I borrowed four hundred from him to buy a car. Fleur insisted. I couldn't even afford to get it on the H.P. I wouldn't have had enough to pay the instalments. I remembered Plaster had once offered another of our fellows the money in similar circumstances. I asked him and he agreed. The car cost four hundred and fifty, second-hand. The rest was interest."

"You never repaid anything?"

"A bit now and then. He didn't seem to mind."

"Was Bastable in his clutches, too?"

"I don't know, but I wouldn't be surprised."

"Why, otherwise, should he want to kill Plaster?"

"I haven't a clue. It's as big a mystery to me as it is to you."

Littlejohn drank up.

"Another?"

"No, thanks. We must go. You'd better come with me to the Yard and make a revised statement. We can't leave things as they are. Ready?"

"Yes. I'd better 'phone Fleur and tell her we're staying

on here a bit. It's nearly ten, though. I'll have to make up a tale of some kind. . . ."

He must have been used to it. He called in the telephone kiosk at the corner by the pub and Littlejohn saw him talking confidently to his wife and even smiling as he talked.

They walked to the car without saying a word, Falconer with his loose gangling strides looking down at the pavement.

" Cigarette? "

They both lit up.

"Is it likely to cause trouble for me, Littlejohn? "

It was the first time he'd addressed the Superintendent that way and it sounded very homely. They might have been friends going for a night out together.

Littlejohn had rather grown to like Falconer. His friendly way, his easygoing tolerance, his calm quizzical outlook on life. There was, too, the slight pathos of the clown in his appearance and the look he gave you. He then remembered Falconer's record in the war, his grim affair with his colleague's wife, the neat and rapid way in which he'd avoided responsibility in the matter of Bastable's suicide. He was no fool, no clown, no pathetic humorist!

They had reached the car.

" I hope I'm not too late back. Fleur'll get worried. . . ."

" Jump in and let's get away then."

It was midnight before it was over and Littlejohn had to drive Falconer home and even help him make excuses to Fleur, who had waited up for him.

14

THE BOOKS OF THE BANK

LITTLEJOHN HAD HARDLY arrived at Scotland Yard next morning before a visitor was announced.

It was Mr. Abbott himself, from the Home Counties, Moorgate.

The bank manager was pale and haggard, as though he hadn't slept all night. He was as sprucely dressed as usual, well-groomed, not a hair out of place, but there were shadows under his eyes and his eyelids were red-rimmed as though he might have been having a good weep.

"We were at the office, Myers and I, last night until past one o'clock. In view of what you said, we decided to go through all the accounts and look for anything peculiar. . . ."

Instead of sending for the usual tea, Littlejohn took out his secret stock of whisky, poured out two helpings, added soda, and passed a glass across to Mr. Abbott.

"You look as if you need a bracer, sir."

"I do. Myers and I kept it dark. We returned after tea when the place was quiet and got out the books. With the exception of the sorry state of poor Bastable's account and, I must say, some of those of other members of the staff. . . ."

Here Mr. Abbott laughed as though it were a stock joke.

". . . we found little to help you, except this. . . ."

He drew from a brief case he was carrying, some loose-leaf account sheets and laid them on the table. They were headed with the name of Frederick Plaster. The manager took a sip of his whisky, looked better for it, strolled to Littlejohn's side of the desk and, leaning over his shoulder, pointed out several items in Plaster's account.

"It may have nothing whatever to do with Bastable, but you'll notice some queer entries in these accounts."

The items to which Mr. Abbott was referring were marked by small crosses in pencil.

"Myers made the crosses. You'll observe that once each month, Plaster drew out a fair sum of money in cash. We've turned-up the cheques, and here they are."

He took a bundle of cheques from his bag, and unfastening the rubber band, spread them fanwise before Littlejohn like a conjuror inviting him to take a card.

They were all payable to *Self*. The entries in the ledger showed withdrawals at varying dates every month, over fifteen months, in rising amounts. Mr. Abbott handed a slip of paper to Littlejohn on which the figures had been taken out.

March 7	£375	Nov. 5	590
April 16	410	Dec. 31	620
May 13	430	Jan. 9	650
June 29	455	Feb. 20	675
July 23	470	Mar. 17	700
Aug. 28	500	Apl. 8	725
Sept. 17	530	May 25	750
Oct. 10	570		

Each cheque was drawn in the same way; in what Mr. Abbott assured Littlejohn was Plaster's own handwriting and figures, and bearing his usual signature. The date only had been inserted by means of a date-stamp.

"Now observe the credit side, Superintendent."

Mr. Abbott ran his finger down the payments to credit over the fifteen months. Among many others, certain figures stood out plainly. Two or three days after each large cheque had been drawn on the account, there was a payment to credit for the same amount as that drawn a few days before.

Mr. Abbott produced the paying-in slips which tallied with the entries. The amounts had been paid-in for credit

of Frederick Plaster at Home Counties Bank, Moorgate
Branch, but the sums, all in one pound notes, had
been received by the United Southern Bank, at South
Mimms.

"We've no branch at South Mimms and Plaster was in
the habit of paying-in at our local agents for his credit
with us."

Mr. Abbott took another drink to keep up his strength.

"It's a queer business, isn't it? But there's one more thing
that's the strangest of all. Myers remembered that I checked
the cash on April 8th, this year. It's his birthday, he was
having a little party at home, and he told me he recollected
how annoyed he was that I'd chosen that date. You see, it
means we're usually an hour later getting away when I take
the cash and, as Myers always assists me, he got home late
for his jollification. . . ."

Mr. Abbott was now much better. The whisky had done
its work and his eyes shone.

"This discovery caused us to compare all the dates with
my private records of cash checking. In every instance but
three, Plaster had drawn the large cheques on the very date
I made my audit. On the dates of the other three, the inspectors from Head Office called and examined the tills. Now,
what do you make of that?"

"I'm bewildered! What does it mean, sir?"

"I confess it baffled me, too. But Myers saw the solution.
Plaster lent Bastable sufficient to put his cash right every
time it was checked!"

"But I thought you said the audit of the tills was done
by surprise. . . ."

Mr. Abbott looked delighted.

"So, it is! But Myers had an answer for that, too. You'll
observe every cheque in this lot is dated with a rubber-
stamped date. It means that Bastable had in his pocket a
cheque, signed by Plaster, for the amount of his cash shortage, for the sum he needed to put it right. I admit he died
with a thousand pounds short in his till. One can only infer
that between the last cheque for £750 on May 25th and the

date he shot himself and we discovered his defalcation,
he must have taken another two hundred and fifty
pounds."

"How did the scheme work?"

"Simple. As soon as Bastable saw me or the inspectors on
our way to control the tills and check their contents with
the books, he used the cheque. Let me explain. . . ."

Mr. Abbott looked at his empty glass, which Littlejohn
refilled with haste.

"The procedure is usually that myself, Carr and Myers,
three officers who have nothing to do with the actual cash,
appear at the counter just after the bank closes on the
chosen afternoon. It is a signal, so to speak, that the
cashiers must at once write-up their counter cash-books,
square them off, and strike their balances of cash under our
close scrutiny. Then we check the balance in figures in
the book with the balance of notes and coin in their tills.
Follow?"

"Yes. . . ."

Littlejohn said it hazily and Abbott was quick to notice.

"The counter cash-book is a simple one. The day is begun
by an item showing the balance of cash the teller had in his
possession when he closed the night before. As the day pro-
gresses, to that balance are added all cash sums paid in to
customers' credit, and from that balance, to put it simply,
are deducted all sums drawn over the counter by clients.
At the end of the day, a new balance is struck, which
should tally with the cash held by the cashier. Now, do you
follow?"

"Yes."

"Carr always took Bastable's cash when we checked it.
Bastable was, let us say, seven hundred pounds wrong on
March 17th. He had Plaster's cheque, undated, in his pocket
for that sum. As soon as Carr arrived for the audit, Bastable
quietly took out the cheque, dated it, and passed it through
his counter cash-book. And, as no cash had been paid out
for it, Bastable's book was now showing a balance equal to
his cash, and was certified as being in order."

"But that meant the connivance of Plaster. Surely, he would never have issued a cheque of such a size without knowing what the money was for."

"He may have done. Bastable might have said he needed the money, let us say for a speculation of some kind and would repay in a day or two. Plaster needn't have known the exact purpose. He doubtless was well-paid for his assistance, for an odd day or so every month. As you see from the pay-ment-in slips, as soon as the monthly cash check was over, Bastable took the amount he'd borrowed and paid it back in cash to Plaster, thus making his till wrong again. No doubt, he paid interest to some tune for the use of it. But, as far as I can see, it saved Plaster having to lend Bastable indefinitely the whole amount necessary to balance his cash. He was only out of his money for, let us say, two days. Then, probably, he gave Bastable another undated cheque for use next time and the whole business started again."

"So that's how the dodge was worked."

"Yes. And, if something else hadn't happened which makes me think differently, we might have discovered the motive for Bastable's taking his own life. You see, when I checked the cash on June 30th, as is invariably the case, because it's half-year end, there would be no cheque to square accounts. Plaster was dead! So Bastable was at his wits' end. It was a good motive for suicide, but. . . ."

Mr. Abbott paused for dramatic effect.

". . . But, when we came to examine Bastable's counter cash-book to make sure our theory was right, no such cheques had been passed through it! And that, in spite of the fact that the paid cheques on Plaster's account indicated that Bastable had dealt with them. You see, when he pays out cash against a cheque, the cashier cancels the drawer's sig-nature by placing his rubber-stamp across the signature. Such stamp bears the name of the bank and a large number as well, which is that of the cashier. In Bastable's case it was Number 2. The cheques drawn by Plaster were stamped No.

2, but they were never passed through Bastable's cash-book!"

"So, he wasn't wrong in his cash?"

"No. But, just to make quite sure nothing had been missed, we looked at the cash-books of the other tellers, as well. All the large cheques, month by month, drawn by Plaster had been passed through *Falconer's* cash-book!"

Mr. Abbott threw out his hands.

"What are we to make of it, Superintendent? The whole business is more baffling than ever."

"Have you mentioned it to Falconer?"

"No. You asked us to be careful and we have been so. I thought I'd better see you first."

"He's no idea you stayed late last night and examined his cash-book?"

"No. Nor have any other members of the staff. Myers and I alone know of it. We even waited until Mrs. Casabon had gone before we began our work. We were completely baffled by the results, I can tell you. I haven't slept all night."

Littlejohn almost said, 'you look it, too,' but he was sorry for Abbott, who seemed to be overwhelmed by the ant-heap of trouble Father Silvester had disturbed.

"Please say nothing, then. Leave matters till this evening and I'll let you know something then."

"Anything else I can do, Littlejohn?"

"Not at present, sir, thanks."

They shook hands and parted. Littlejohn at once rang for a plain-clothes officer, described Falconer to him, and told him to keep an eye on him until further notice. He once thought of sending him in the bank to change a five-pound note and thus get a better look at Falconer, but as the officer, a good and worthy constable, had *police* written all over him from head to foot, he thought there wasn't any sense in alarming his quarry.

Then, he telephoned Father Silvester.

"Sorry to trouble you, Father, but could you bring over Christine Bobbitt again, if she's still in circulation?"

Twenty minutes later the cassock and the matadors crossed the road to Scotland Yard.

Christine had evidently mutely obeyed the priest's instructions to follow him, as usual, but when she reached the Yard, she had plenty to say to Littlejohn.

"What's the game? Me keep bein' seen comin' to Scotland Yard'll do me no good. It'll get round I'm a friend of the police."

She obviously didn't relish the relationship. Her face expressed extreme disgust.

"Sit down, Christine, and speak when you're spoken to."

"Yes, but. . . ."

The priest pointed to a chair and she was silent. She sat dangling her legs and chewing her gum, quite unperturbed by her surroundings.

"I won't keep you long, Father. I've just a question or two to ask Miss Bobbitt. . . ."

He said it deliberately and she was quick to take him up.

"Not so much of your Miss Bobbitt! "

The priest had evidently picked her up in all her glory in the street, for the mascara was around her eyes again and her lips were thickly daubed with red, which clashed with the colour of her jeans. The incongruous thing about her was that she was wearing a teddy-boy's jacket, several sizes too large for her. When Father Silvester encountered her, she had been wearing a thin sleeveless blouse with little on beneath it, and the priest had stopped one of her male companions, borrowed his jacket, and insisted on her putting it on. This she did with great pleasure, for he was a boy she fancied, and the voluptuous warmth of the body he had just removed from it remained behind to stimulate her queer fancies. She hugged the jacket to her in ecstasy.

"Well, Christine. . . . I just want to ask you if you'd recognize the man who threw the body in the canal on the night you and Alfie were there together, if you saw him again."

Christine nonchalantly chewed her quid of gum.

"I said I never saw him. I was left behind in the long grass."

"I don't believe it, Christine. When we were out together the other evening, you were so inquisitive that you couldn't keep still. Wandering about *The Bargees' Rest* and the wharf. Don't ask me to believe you didn't follow Alfie to see what he was at that night."

"Believe what you like. I told you. . . ."

"That will do!"

The priest had decided to take a hand.

"Did you, or did you not see the man the Superintendent speaks of, on the night you were with Alfie? Now the truth, or I'll put you across my knee and slap the daylights out of you!"

Christine gave him a slow inviting smile as though she'd enjoy a bit of rough handling by someone who really was a man.

"I think I sorta. . . ." she said finally.

"You sorta! Speak properly. Did you see him?"

"Yep."

"Why lie about it, then?"

"It's against me principles to get a man in trouble with the p'lice."

"Even if he's a murderer?"

"I thought the body was dead."

"Never mind what you thought. Now, do as the Superintendent asks, and keep a civil tongue in your head."

She didn't seem to understand half of what he was saying, but she knew he was angry with her.

"If he hadn't been a parson, I could fall for 'im in a big way," she often told her girl friends.

"What 'ave I to do?"

"Come with me and identify him," said Littlejohn.

"Not likely!"

"You'll come, Christine. You've only to stand with me near where he'll appear and tell me if that's the man you saw."

"Will *he* come, too?"

As though, somehow, the huge priest would protect her from the danger the word *murder* had bred in her mind.

"Yes."

"Where do we go to? I want to get home. I gotta date."

"We're going to the City in a car."

"What are we waitin' for?"

It was lunch-time—ten past twelve—and Falconer went for his meal at one. Littlejohn shepherded the pair of them downstairs to a police-car and they were driven to Moorgate.

Opposite the Home Counties Bank stood a pub which served snack lunches with pints of beer. The upstairs room had a window facing the bank. Luckily, the place wasn't yet crowded and they found a seat at a small table overlooking the street.

"Makes you hungry, don't it?" said Christine, eyeing the cold fare on the counter.

Littlejohn ordered some beef sandwiches and two beers.

"A bitter-lemon for her ladyship," said Father Silvester.

Christine prepared for the feed by sticking her gum under the table.

They had almost finished their meal when Falconer appeared at the door of the bank. He had an unlit cigarette in his mouth and paused to ask for a light from a man leaning against a lamp standard reading a racing paper. The man obliged and Falconer gave him a knowing smile. It was Littlejohn's constable! As his quarry made for the City, the plain-clothes man fell in step at a respectable distance behind him, trying to make himself as inconspicuous as possible, even pulling down the brim of his soft hat, as though, somehow, it would screen him from view from the man ahead.

"That's him!"

Christine didn't even need to be asked. As Littlejohn peered through the window, she took a drink of his beer.

"I could do with a few more of those," she said, indicating the sandwiches. "An' a sausage or two and some potato crisps."

Littlejohn obliged with the lot and she settled down to demolish them. After which, she rescued her gum, put it in its usual place, and intimated that she'd got a date.

"You're sure the man you saw was the one who threw the body in the canal on the night . . . ? "

"I said it was, didn't I? I can't say more. What do you want me to do? Cross me heart and all that. . . ."

"You may be called upon to give evidence in court. I'll let you know if that becomes necessary. It may not be."

He'd expected a lot more protests and impertinence. Instead of which, Christine almost rubbed against him like a purring cat.

"If I do that, will you pay for me a good slap-up meal, like the one you just give me? "

"Yes."

"Promise? "

"It's a deal."

She allowed herself to be led away quietly by Father Silvester, who, however, insisted on a taxi.

"I refuse to walk through London with anybody dressed-up like this little ragamuffin. It might be Guy Fawkes night, and you the Guy, Christine Bobbitt."

Littlejohn had heard the men at *The Bargees' Rest* speak of their favourite pubs in London, and Falconer had mentioned both *The Green Man* and *The Grapes*. He called at both. In the second, the detective-constable detailed to keep an eye on Falconer was sitting at a table, still reading his paper. When his eye fell on Littlejohn he tried to look as if he didn't know him.

"Looking for me, Superintendent? "

It was Falconer, sitting alone, with a pint of beer on the table before him. His head was resting on the leather back of his seat; his long legs sprawled in front of him. Now and then, someone almost fell over them, but he didn't move them. "Sorry," he said. The same bored, cheerful expression, the same clownish look, and the bright humorous eyes.

"Think we might get rid of my shadow, Littlejohn? "

He jerked his head sadly in the direction of the plain-clothes man and gave Littlejohn a reproachful Bimbo look as if to say " I expected better from you ".

Falconer snapped his fingers at the waiter. He looked almost too tired to raise his arm to do it.

" Bring me another, and one for my friend. . . ."

He asked no questions about why Littlejohn was there.

" How's things, Littlejohn? "

" All right, Alec."

He used Falconer's Christian name quite naturally. He was the kind of man you grew to like.

The shadow was folding-up his paper and looking ready to go at the slightest hint. He was an efficient officer who had worked with Littlejohn before, but he was far too fussy. He mistook it for diligence and hoped to gain promotion by it. His name was Askew.

Littlejohn crossed to him.

" That'll be all, thank you, Askew. I'll look after things now."

" He's not armed. I bumped against him twice. Once on each side. Nothing."

He said it quietly out of the corner of his mouth.

" Thank you very much, Askew."

" Had I better stick around in case he proves awkward? "

" He won't. See you later."

" Good-bye, sir."

He looked as if he felt that the next time they met, Littlejohn might be on the slab in the morgue.

Falconer was drinking yet another pint. He was as steady as a rock, too. No question of pushing him down the bank's coal-hole later, like the late Mr. Lett.

" It's time I was getting back, Littlejohn. But I guess this time, it doesn't really matter, does it? "

" No, Alec, it doesn't matter about the bank any more."

Falconer nodded placidly.

" Nothing seems to matter any more, now. Fleur went away this morning. Or perhaps I ought to say *ran* away with her lover. He's a parson. . . ."

He laughed good humouredly, as though he'd read about it in a book.

" Good health! "

Littlejohn gently lifted his tankard.

" Good health, Alec."

15

AT *THE GRAPES*

THERE WERE MEN drinking beer and eating sandwiches all over the room. Brokers in bowlers, solicitors in their black jackets and grey trousers, jobbers without hats, bankmen happily talking banking, as usual. . . . Some were just back from holidays, sunburned and making a lot of fuss about the places where they'd been staying. At the buffet, a perspiring man was slicing ham, tongue and cold beef with convulsive movements. Last year, he had won the catering society's prize for the most rapid making of sandwiches. . . .

Littlejohn was only dimly conscious of what was going on. Falconer was talking in his drawling hollow voice.

"Sorry, Littlejohn. Hope you don't mind. I've got to tell somebody. It's so damned funny."

"Don't apologize. Get it off your chest, Alec. It'll do you good."

"As I was saying, right from being a kid, Fleur's loved Gus. They're cousins and were brought-up together. He was a deeply religious chap as a young man, but he couldn't finally make up his mind what he believed and what he didn't. He started as a Methodist, like the rest of his family. Then he turned Catholic and decided to become a priest. That did it. They'd all thought Gus and Fleur would make a match of it. I think she took me on the rebound. . . . Or, it might have been pity. . . ."

He emptied his tankard and signalled for two more.

"After Fleur and I were married, Gus changed again. This time it was Christian Science or Theosophy, I forget which. He went to Australia. He wrote to Fleur regularly. I was never allowed to read his letters. If he'd asked her to marry him, I'm sure Fleur would have divorced me after the Irma affair and cleared off. But he didn't believe in divorce at that stage of his religious development. Now, he does. He's turned atheist because of the atom bomb. I don't know his philosophic train of thought in that direction. What matters to me is that a couple of days ago, he returned from Australia, Fleur's gone to her brother's, and the next thing, there will be divorce papers, I expect. She left a note on the table and just went. I hope she knows what she's doing. He might easily decide on the priesthood again, or even become a Mormon. He's that sort. Then, where would Fleur be?"

He smiled. It might have been a discussion of a theoretical case far removed from his own affairs.

"But you've something you want to ask me, I think, Little-john?"

He spoke as though some kind of reaction had set-in, now. His voice was toneless. He sounded down for the count, licked.

"I know about the cash deficiency, Alec. It was you, not Bastable, who was a thousand short, wasn't it? When he shot himself you saw a chance to save yourself and you took it. You switched a thousand from his cash to your own. You were really seven-fifty wrong, but you took the extra two-fifty for luck."

Falconer gave him a disappointed look.

"Not for luck, old boy, please. I hadn't time to count out seven hundred and fifty from the loose notes. I took two made-up bundles of five hundred each . . . unused ones. I suppose that extra two-fifty puzzled you a bit."

"It did. You'd carried the cash deficiency a long time, too, by means of Plaster's cheques. Did he know what the cheques were for?"

Falconer lit a cigarette and fixed his eyes on a bright reflection in his tankard. It made him squint a bit.

"Not at first. I said it was for stock exchange speculations on tips I'd been given. He swallowed it. Finally, I think he tumbled to it. How did you know? From his bank account, I guess. I was a bit troubled about the scheme myself. There was a wide-open flaw in it. You see, the cheques had to go through *my* cash-book. It could have been spotted by anyone suspicious. However, Bastable might have been trying to make things easy for me. His domestic misery, his poverty, and then the gun going off exactly as though it were suicide instead of an accident, even to the way it was found gripped in his hands. He was inoffensive to the last. Even died without a murmur."

"Yes. You could sneak his counter-stamp from under his very nose and put his No. 2. on the cheques, but they had to go through *your* book to square your discrepancies. Poor Bastable's suicide made everybody sure it was he who was wrong in his cash and they didn't check the books for tricks."

"You seem to know all about it. Who tumbled to it?"

"Myers."

"He's a wizard at figures. I thought it might be he. I was half afraid before you came into the affair at all, that Myers would rumble me. Luckily, he was so upset by Bastable's death. They were buddies in spite of Bastable's eternal whining. Myers is absolutely stolid and loyal."

"What made you start it all, Alec? Were you hard-up?"

"Always. Fleur came from a family with money. Although her father was a parson, her mother once had a private fortune but it almost petered out during the troubles in the wool trade. Until she married me, she'd never gone short of anything she wanted. And Gus inherited the estates of what seemed to be dozens of maiden aunts. Every time one died, Fleur would sigh, 'She'll have left it all to Gus,'—and she had. He's a tall, anaemic, bony chap, is Gus, and yet the women seem to go for him in a big way. They must want to mother him! One day, when I've time, I'll write an essay on sex-appeal. Pity I didn't introduce him to Irma. The pair of them together would have gone up in smoke! Where was I? Was I hard-up? Yes. I've always had the tastes of a tycoon myself."

Which was true. His suit was obviously by an expensive tailor. His tie and shirt looked to be from the best makers, and his shoes were hand-made.

He chanted on, like a lamenting philosopher.

"I got among the wrong lot in the war. Rich Frenchmen. They undermined my economy for ever."

"You borrowed from Plaster?"

"Yes. And I paid him back when, finally, he threatened if I didn't repay, he'd tell Abbott I'd been borrowing from him. That's one of the most hideous crimes in a bank; borrowing from a customer. I had to have the money or lose my job. I took it from my till. The hard cash pleased Plaster no end. He softened off and said I could borrow again from time to time, if I wanted. He lent me the cheques after that and I returned the money in cash after I'd used them to evade the monthly cash-check. You've learned of how it was wangled, I expect. Otherwise, you wouldn't be here."

"Yes."

"Myers again?"

"Yes."

A bitter smile.

"I guess the bank will prosecute me, now. *I'm* alive. I didn't shoot myself, so I can't hope for mercy."

"It's more than that, Alec. It's murder."

At first, Falconer said nothing. His shoulders drooped a bit more and he drew in his legs as though he might be preparing to make a run for it.

"What do you mean, murder, Littlejohn?"

"You were seen at Waterbury Wharf, Alec. You shouldn't have told me the tale about Bastable borrowing your car that night. . . ."

"But, he did! That's the funny part. He always seemed anxious to oblige. When he'd gone, I told Fleur I was going out for a drink. Instead, I took a bus to South Mimms to see Plaster. I'd evaded the cash-check again that day by using Plaster's cheque, as usual, and I was due to refund the money in pound notes. He was drunk and in the shop alone. He was awkward. I should have left him and tackled him again when he was sober. It would have been all right, then. Instead, I argued. He said he was sure I was fiddling some way at the bank. One thing led to another, and then he said something offensive about Fleur. I'd been feeling like killing him for what he'd suspected about the fiddle. Now, I hit him hard. It was the kind of blow we used in the Underground in the war. With the side of the hand, you know. It leaves no marks as a rule. He fell like a log. . . . What about some more beer? "

He flapped his hand at the waiter.

" Two more."

They were sitting alone. All the lunchtime crowd had melted away and the landlord and staff were clearing-up and having their meals. The barman was eating a large pie in his fingers and the sandwich champion was slowly cutting himself a round of cold beef.

" I don't know what happened. He fell, and when I came to examine him, he wasn't breathing. I was in a fix. Then, I thought of the canal and the deserted wharf at Waterbury. I must confess I lost my nerve a bit. I should have left him where he was and crept off. Instead, I felt a compulsion to get rid of the body. A stupid trick. It was my undoing. Plaster's car was at the door. I got him under my arm. He was a little chap and not much weight. I dandled him to the car, looking as if I were helping out a drunk. I even talked to him, in case anybody should see us. There was nobody about, because it was half-closing day and I guess Mrs. Plaster was sweethearting somewhere with her boyfriend. I took Plaster and tipped him in the canal."

He took a swig of his beer and gave a deep sigh as though he were enjoying it.

" Damn me, if my luck still didn't hold! Plaster mustn't have been quite dead. In my haste, I hadn't noticed he was breathing slightly. Result, he drowned. And the medical evidence at the coroner's court was according. His bellyful of alcohol led to the idea that he'd fallen in when he was drunk. I didn't mind drowning him, at all. I was sick of him. He was a no-good and he stood there, drunk and filthy, and suggested I could have the money if I'd put-in a good word for him with Fleur. . . . I ought to have throttled him instead of just hitting him. It almost made me retch. . . ."

He made a revolving gesture with his forefinger as he held his tankard in the other hand.

"But my luck still held. You see, just before Abbott checked the cash again for the half-year end, Bastable had his little accident and I was able to get the cash from *his* till and square myself. Otherwise, without Plaster and his cheque, I'd have been sunk."

"You took Plaster's car home afterwards?"

"Yes. I garaged it whilst I went indoors and put on a hat and a raincoat. It disguised me a bit, that. Hid the bald head and my way of walking. Bastable wasn't back. Fortunate again. I took out Plaster's car after dark and left it with the lights on. He must have done the same thing pretty often, for next morning the car had gone. Presumably his missus garaged it when she came home with her herbalist. It was a perfect crime till you turned-up."

"But the teddy-boy and his girl were watching, hidden in the long grass. They saw it all, Alec. The girl recognized you as you left the bank to come here today."

"Yes. The teddy-boy paid me a call and started his little blackmail stunt. I'd have thought no more of killing him than I did of Plaster. A little pest and a no-good, too. Then, he vanished."

"Yes. He read in the paper about a cashier at your branch in Moorgate committing suicide. He thought it was you, Alec, and that you'd done it on account of his threats. He kept away for a bit and then he decided, when the heat had gone off, to check up. He daren't risk calling at the bank, or he was too cautious to try it. But he knew you both frequented *The Bargees' Rest*, because in his enthusiasm to get to know how much you were worth and what you did in your spare time, he'd followed you there. He went and spied round at the *Rest* and found you still alive and kicking. That night, he died. You were lucky again. But before he died, he told a priest—not very clearly, I'm afraid, for he was only half-conscious—all about the Waterbury Wharf affair and the blackmail. I got involved. The thing that kept me going was the thousand pounds. I couldn't rest till I'd found out what Bastable did with it. It led me to you, Alec."

For a time, neither of them spoke. There was something dogged and obstinate in Falconer's silence, as though he refused now to be drawn further, or else hoped some loophole in the logic of it all would appear.

" Good health ! " he said at length as he took a drink from the last tankard he'd been served and which had been standing waiting at his elbow.

" It's a funny business, isn't it? It all began with Irma. She ruined Bastable. Then, she ruined me, although it was a kind of slow-motion ruin in my case. Even now, I haven't properly got her out of my blood. Like drugs or alcohol. If she'd wanted me back, she'd only need to raise her little finger, and I couldn't help myself. I've been hers, in a manner of speaking, ever since we met."

" You mean to say you really fell in love with her? "

" I guess I did."

He said it casually and nodded. No emotion, no sentiment. Just a plain statement of fact.

" She'll not stick with Peppercorn. You'll see. Ever since we broke it off, she's never stuck to anybody for long."

Now, Falconer was kidding himself. This was the weak spot in his armour. It accounted for his boredom, his heavy drinking, his dismal existence. His affair with Irma was his one big purple patch in life and he clung to it like one who remembers a happy dream until he believes it actually happened.

" Fleur will be happy, at last. I've never been any good for her. We weren't suited from the start. I thought I could perhaps make her love me. . . . I've given her a rough time. We were both bored stiff with each other in the end. I certainly was browned-off with her and her eternal Gus. All those blasted souvenirs in the house came from him, sent to her as he travelled in all parts of the world, seeking the light, as he called it. Well, now, for the time being, at least, he's an atheist. He's walked right into the dark. Like me."

Littlejohn slowly lit his pipe without glancing at Falconer. He was sure he was looking more like a broken-hearted clown than ever.

Falconer folded his arms and leaned his head wearily on the wall behind. He was smiling again. It upset Littlejohn. They'd been friends whilst the mystery lasted and now Alec had reached the end.

" Will they hang me? "

" No. But you'll get a fair stretch, even if they agree that Plaster's death was manslaughter. In any case, it won't be capital punishment. As for the cash shortage, that rests with the bank. They probably won't go on with it in view of the other charge."

Falconer lit another cigarette and drew in the smoke voluptuously. It might have been his last, the way he enjoyed it.

" I'm due to retire soon. Without Fleur, I might as well spend the time in gaol. I hear they've cosy beds, flowers in the cells, libraries, tobacco, even holidays for the good boys. I may not get as much beer as I'd like, but I'll have to bring myself to manage without it. They may even have a kind of *Bargees' Rest* where we're sent to now and then by way of a change."

He sounded slightly contemptuous, but humorous still.

" After France, and my days with Irma, my life's just seemed colourless. Squalid, if you get what I mean. It wasn't Fleur's fault; my own entirely. Lucky the teddy-boy died like he did. I'd certainly have had to kill him. Can't put-up with blackmail. Who's the girl, by the way? "

" A teddy-girl called Christine."

" Incongruous name, isn't it? Well, I suppose this is the finish. When I come out, if I ever do, I'll be getting on for seventy. My God! Seventy! I'll have to go in an institution for old lags, then, I guess. Everybody will have forgotten me."

His mouth twisted as though he'd taken a dose of nasty medicine.

Just a hopeless, dreary future. It even lacked drama. The

sordid, futile, desolate existence of a man without hope and who'd mismanaged everything. . . .

And yet, Littlejohn couldn't help thinking that Falconer hadn't lost all his dignity. He was fundamentally a simple man who'd been fooled and led away by everybody. The very counterpart in real life of the clown in a circus. Irma, the cheap adventuress, with her promiscuousness, her mania for banal affairs, her reek of scent, her voluptuous physical equipment. She'd made Falconer think he was the only man in her life.

Bastable had attached himself to him, sponging and whining, and made him pay for his fun with his wife. And Plaster had played him along with private loans at extortionate interest and had the nerve to covet Fleur.

Even Fleur had married him out of spite because Gus had left her in the lurch and preferred his religion. Now, having used Falconer as a breadwinner for years, she was back with Gus. . . .

Falconer had lost his troubled look. He seemed like someone who'd found rest, an end to it all. In the peace of prison! Even better off than Gus, who couldn't settle down to a single belief or consolation! He'd come out of it all better than his tormentors. Nothing to hide, nobody to pester him and sponge on him, reading his eternal Proust in his cell. Perhaps he'd be prison librarian one day! And when he came out, at last, the welfare state would look after him!

Meanwhile, Irma would continue the dreary round until she ended in the gutter or some man pinned her down, at length, like a butterfly on a card. Plaster and Bastable were dead. Fleur would have to put up with the temperamental Gus, perpetually weathercocking his way through a religious mania of queer doubts and faiths. . . . And Falconer would be safe in gaol. . . .

" And you climbed out through the coal-hole, Alec? "

He didn't know why he said it, but it seemed to bring the whole affair down to earth.

' You even knew that, too, Littlejohn! You're a wizard! "